The Foxhall-Trott Pupil

Maurice C Chinnick

First published 2024
by Rowanvale Books Ltd
The Gate
Keppoch Street
Roath
Cardiff
CF24 3JW
www.rowanvalebooks.com

A CIP catalogue record for this book is available from the British Library.

ISBN: 978-1-83584-004-7
eBook ISBN: 978-1-83584-003-0

To my beautiful wife Gill, who has always encouraged and supported me throughout, no matter what obstacles we faced.

To our remarkable and thoughtful son Julian, his wonderful, supportive wife Kate and our grandchildren, Holly and Sienna, who give us so much pleasure.

To Holly's fiancé, Nick, and our beautiful great-granddaughter Athena.

Contents

CHAPTER 1
IN THE BEGINNING

Location:
A working-class area within an industrial/maritime city in the UK.

Period:
Post-WWII, during the 1940/50s.

Main Character:
Tomas Larsen. His family and school friends call him Tom.

Background:
Tom was brought up by his paternal grandfather, Frederik, and widowed aunt, Anja.

This is a story about Tom's journey through his younger years and into adulthood, by overcoming prejudice and ignorance.

SCHOOL YEARS

SISTER MARY MICHAEL'S CLASS: Reception–Year 2
These early school years are still vivid in Tom's memory. The school's inner corridor doors were shut as soon as the school bell rang. Seconds late, and you were held behind these closed doors until prayers were finished.

Tom's mind would be racing, imagining what punishment would be dealt out to the four-year-olds by certain nuns, with their long black habits and piercing cold eyes behind rimless glasses. Their mission was only completed when they saw tears roll down these children's cheeks and plop onto their shirts or blouses.

The school's catchment area of the City's docks encompassed a small enclave of descendants of the Irish immigrants who'd been brought over from Ireland during 1840/50s to help build the docks. This small enclave contributed considerable funds to both the school and church, even though many of the families were considered to be on the breadline.

During these very early years, Tom started to encounter prejudice. He soon learnt that children with certain family names who contributed funds to the school were brought to the front of the class and their questions and queries were given more attention. The children from Northern Europe, the Mediterranean and the Caribbean were dispatched to the rear of the class and told to put their hand down when they had a question. They had to hope their query would eventually be raised by pupils in the front.

During musical sessions, instruments were given to the same few pupils, while the remainder of the class just had to clap in time.

Tom had to endure three years in the nuns' clutches, before going up to the next class.

MISS AMELIA PRATT'S CLASS: Year 3–4
The start of a new school year.

As the classroom door opened, everybody's eyes were fixed upon on it.

In walked a rather tall, slim elderly lady with grey hair rolled up around the edges and held in place with hairgrips. She had a wide smile right across her face.

Tom watched her eyes slowly scan right around the classroom like a pair of searchlights, taking in the various coloured skin tones, hair textures and facial features.

All the faces just lit up with joy because she was not wearing a black habit.

"Good morning, children. My name is Miss Amelia Pratt, and I would be obliged if you all called me Miss Pratt," she said in a clear but soft voice.

Her attire consisted of a floral duster coat over a crisp white blouse, with a silk floral scarf around her neck to match her duster. A lace handkerchief was tucked into the cuff of her coat.

Her straight, plain skirt finished just below the knee, trimming the edge of thick, flesh-coloured stockings that travelled down to a well-polished pair of laced-up kitten-heeled shoes. Her eyes were light brown; she had a fair complexion and wore no makeup.

"I see that I have a wonderful mixture of pupils who, in one way or another, have come from different parts of the world," she said. "Right, I have a few golden rules that I want you to follow.

"**One**: When I am speaking or when you are carrying out a task, no chattering whatsoever.

"**Two**: When I put a question to the class, you will put your hand up if you think you know the answer. I will then ask you for your response. If incorrect I will move on to another pupil.

"**Three**: Anybody—and I mean anybody—caught sniggering or laughing, if a pupil gets the answer wrong will be brought out to the front of the class and given the most difficult question to try and answer.

"**Four**: To ensure that every pupil can hear my dulcet tones, every Monday morning, the children that were sat in the back row shall move to the front. The front row shall move to the row behind. There are four rows; therefore, we shall rotate the class seating every four weeks."

Tom liked all these rules; they were fair to everybody.

Miss Pratt was a great believer in the Chinese proverb by Confucius: "The man who asks a question is a fool for a minute, a man who does not ask is a fool for a lifetime."

She first went around the class asking everybody in turn their name and where their family originally came from. Tom's heart immediately sank as he thought that the same prejudices were now going to start all over again, but he could not have been further from the truth.

The pupils gave an ever-growing list of countries that their parents or grandparents had come from: Jamaica, Wales, Ireland, Malta, Italy, Greece, Denmark, Norway, Spain—the list went on. Great Britain had a serious labour shortage after WWII, and migrants had come from all parts of the world.

Some children were third and fourth generation, as their city was a busy seaport. Sailors stayed and married local women.

A small brass push bell sat on the corner of Miss Pratt's desk. She used it to call for silence when there was too much chattering.

"Now that we know what different parts of the world your fellow pupils' parents or grandparents have come from, we shall learn about their customs and culture. Therefore, each pupil will be told a week in advance to prepare a short script and read it out to the class, covering things such as what type of food their family eat, are there any special dishes for certain occasions, any special days they celebrate, et cetera."

To Tom, this seemed like a brilliant way to break down barriers and to get to know more about his fellow pupils, like why different pupils ate certain foods. He had often heard women gathered in a huddle talking in an unkind way about certain families they'd seen carrying an expensive bag of fruit, meat or fish (food was still being rationed, and would be until 1954). Through the other pupils' presentations, the class learned that those families would go without lots of other foods throughout the week and save up their ration coupons for months just to have that one luxury item that would remind them of their homeland. It was the equivalent of Christian families putting a little aside each week or month towards Christmas festivities.

With hindsight, Tom realised Miss Amelia Pratt knew exactly what she was doing. She was bringing pupils of different backgrounds, customs and cultures closer together.

Miss Pratt had travelled quite extensively to various parts of Europe as well as the Mediterranean, North Africa and the Middle East during the interwar years. She would always set aside a few hours each week to tell the class about her travels and the various people she had met. There was always some keepsake from those countries relating to her story that she would pass around the class. Tom thought this was a wonderful way of learning about the different countries, the people and their customs. On many occasions a pupil would make reference to the fact that their family lived in that part of the world or that their parent or grandparent had a similar object on display in their house to remind them of their homeland.

Miss Pratt made everybody feel that they were all part of the same world, even though there are different countries, customs and cultures.

Her approach to the various subjects she taught was to explain them so that most pupils fully understood. If a pupil didn't, she would always ask if another pupil would like to help that person during break time, but she was always on hand to help.

When teaching mathematics, she would encourage the pupils to learn different ways to calculate their answers. In one particular lesson, she instructed each pupil to measure the width of one of their classmate's shoulders, the length of their arms and from their neck to the bottom of their pullover or cardigan, making sure the pupil being measured was clearly identified on the top of the page. Mathematical lessons were then taught by using the pupils' measurements in different formats. This was much more fun to Tom than traditional ways.

Miss Amelia Pratt also had another motive for this measuring exercise. She lived alone, and one of her pastimes was listening to the radio while knitting. During her lessons, she would observe various pupils' clothes and when she saw that a child's knitwear item had gone well beyond the excessive darning stage, she would pull out that pupil's measurements. She would select a colour and pattern that she thought would suit that boy or girl, and with that pupil's measurements in front of her, she would knit a sweater or cardigan for the pupil, allowing a little extra for growth. The finished product would then be parcelled up in brown paper, secured with white string, and the knots of the string sealed with red wax to prevent accidental or intentional opening by the pupil before it reached home.

The delivery of the parcel to the pupil was done with the utmost discretion. The pupil would be asked to stay behind after lessons to discuss some work; the package would then be handed to the pupil with the most direct instructions to the pupil and the family not to tell anyone where the gift came from. The gifts were always most welcome, as money was tight and clothes were on ration.

Friday afternoon was one of Tom's favourite times. This was storytelling time. Miss Pratt was brilliant at reading stories from children's books. Tom would wait in anticipation when Miss Pratt took a small key from her desk drawer and place it into the lock of the wooden-framed bookcase. He would watch her fingers travel along the bookshelf, wondering where they would stop. Would it be one of his favourite stories, or another that hadn't been read to them yet? All eyes would be on the book's dust jacket, trying to read the title. Miss Pratt always put a page marker in the book to mark where they'd finished last time she read to them.

The ritual began with the two pupils, designated via a rota system, who carried a high, wooden chair made of pine with a relatively short upright back to the centre of the classroom, directly in front of Miss Pratt's desk. She raised herself up onto the chair and wriggled into a comfortable reading position. The pupils did exactly the same in their seats.

Tom would then be ready for an hour or so of absolute delight, waiting for the magical experience to unfold. Miss Pratt could lift the characters from the page and float them around the classroom just by altering the tone and pitch of her voice, including theatrical pauses, when needed.

At the end there was always a plea for more, but Miss Pratt would close the book and say, "We will carry on with it next week." These storytelling moments were a catalyst for Tom's hunger for knowledge and reading.

Tom spent two glorious years in the company of this wonderful lady who demonstrated so much fairness and equality. Even at his young age, she gave Tom the tools to explore and self-educate.

The end of the last term with Miss Pratt was a true finale.

Throughout the year, she had monitored the work and progress of her pupils. At the end of the year, she gave out three main prizes: top of the class, second, and best progress.

Monica Xereb, a pretty Maltese girl, won first prize which consisted of a postal order to the value of 2s/6d. Second prize was won by Connor Murphy from the small enclave of Irish immigrants. He received a postal order to the value of 1s/6d. There was a loud applause for each prize winner.

You could have heard a pin drop when waiting for the best progress award to be announced.

"The winner of the best progress award goes to Tomas Larsen," Miss Pratt announced.

Tom had a smile from ear to ear. He walked up to receive his prize. It was a book called *My Garden Shed*. He was delighted to have this award, because written inside the cover was a message from Miss Pratt which read:

This book is awarded to Tomas Larsen for conquering all challenges and tasks throughout the term and his unwavering support to his fellow pupils.

Miss Amelia Pratt, Form Teacher 1948.

MR JOHN RYAN'S CLASS: Year 5–6

This was the first year that Tom had a male teacher; his name was Mr John Ryan. He was of average height with straight, black, greying hair, and his skin was quite pale. He wore a crisp white shirt with a tie that had college symbols and colours. The shirt cuffs were closed by a pair of silver cufflinks. Bright red braces held up a pair of thick tweed trousers with turn-ups at the bottom. His socks were bright red to match his braces, and his leather shoes shone with oxblood-red shoe polish. His jacket, placed over the back of his chair, was also tweed but did not match the trousers. On the elbows were large leather patches.

"Well, well, well, what have we here," was his opening remark to the class. "Miss Pratt has informed me that you are an excellent class to teach. I have a record of your names and family backgrounds, supplied by Miss Pratt, but I need to put a face to each name.

"Starting with you"—he pointed to Mario—"and travelling in that direction, stand up and give me your name."

As the pupils did so, every now and again, Mr Ryan would nod and say "Good", and at the end of the roll call he gave a large smile and said, "Give yourselves a round of applause for getting your names right."

This brought a titter of laughter from around the classroom. Tom had a good feeling about Mr Ryan.

"I have the same routine as Miss Pratt," Mr Ryan explained. "Each Monday morning, those of you seated in the front row will move to the row behind, and so on.

"You are all in my special team and I am your coach. My job is to try and get all of you to win Part I and Part II of the eleven-plus exams, to ensure you all have a bright future ahead of you."

Passing this exam would give a child entry to a grammar school, providing a higher standard of education than a secondary modern or comprehensive school.

"Right, open those windows to get fresh air in to feed our brains, and now I want you to all learn the 'jelly shake'."

With that, Mr Ryan rolled his shirtsleeves up to his elbows and started to shake from his shoulders to his feet. There were howls of laughter as the pupils mimicked him. This lasted for about two minutes.

"We will do that each morning before lessons," Mr Ryan explained.

Tom wondered what the purpose of the two large brass hooks on the wall directly behind where Mr Ryan sat was. He saw Tom looking at these, so he called him out to his desk and asked him to choose another pupil to help him with a small task.

"Underneath my desk you will find a rolled-up banner," he said. "I want you and Desmond to unfurl it and hang it on those hooks."

The banner read:

WE ALL PRAISE AND ENCOURAGE EACH OTHER, BECAUSE WE ARE A TEAM.

Mr Ryan drilled them in the core subjects required to achieve a pass in the eleven-plus exam: verbal reasoning, non-verbal reasoning, mathematics and English. He advised the class that past papers of previous exams could be obtained from well-established bookshops at a cost of one shilling per subject. He suggested that they should obtain at least the past three years' papers.

Mr Ryan knew in his heart that this wasn't possible. The area was very poor.

This expenditure would have cost a family several meals for the whole week and was therefore completely out of reach for most, if not all, of the pupils within his class. Unfortunately, the public library did not hold these papers.

Mr Ryan and his pupils ploughed on with any past papers Mr Ryan could obtain. Some came from his former friends at the teacher training college.

ELEVEN-PLUS EXAM DAY:

The room was full of nervous giggles and chatter, the sound of pencils and wooden rulers being positioned. The pupils' ink pens were wooden and had disposable nibs which were dipped into brown ceramic inkwells, hollowed into the desks.

"Right," said Mr Ryan. "We are going to start the exam in five minutes. Please make sure your inkwell is full, your pen nib is clean and your pencil is sharp. As we have practiced many times, the whole exam lasts for sixty minutes. This only allows you to spend at most fifteen minutes on each subject. I will tell you when you have only five minutes left for each subject."

After a silenced hush, Mr Ryan said, "You may turn your papers over and begin."

There were various sighs, coughs and the rapid turning over of paper as students tried to figure out which question to tackle first.

Mr Ryan called out the timing schedule throughout the exam. Then, with a loud crack from a wooden ruler that he slapped down hard on the desk, he called out "Time! Pens down." There was a loud exhale of breath across the classroom.

Sadly, Tom did not pass this exam, which students only had one chance to succeed at. He was not going to attend a grammar school, but an all-boys secondary modern, which in his opinion was an establishment intended to teach enough basic education to enter factory or construction work. This was not how he saw his future.

During the summer holidays, the pupils moving up to the secondary modern school heard rumours about the quirks and tolerances of the teachers from older siblings and friends who attended the school. Each pupil was already making a mental note of his first choice as form master.

CHAPTER 2
SECONDARY MODERN SCHOOL

The secondary modern school brought together boys from all over the City. It was a cauldron for making new friends, but also new enemies.

Tom's school was in what was considered to be a rather tough area. Boys from the more well-heeled part of the City kept their distance.

The teachers also had their own personal challenges, although the challenge for them was probably more about who could climb the greasy pole the quickest to become deputy head or the head of a department.

It was said that the headmaster, Edwin Lombard-Stoat, was selected because of his skill in dealing with children that had challenging behaviour.

He was tall, rather thin, with greased-back black hair parted down the centre. His sharp, pointed nose displayed a pencil-thin black moustache beneath it, while his complexion was grey to match his waistcoated, pinstriped suit. His bony fingers would twist together as if wringing out a wet towel when he spoke.

Most of the teachers were pretty much nonplussed about their attire. Their jackets and blazers looked as though they were pre-owned, covering white or checked shirts and ties. Their trousers had plenty of creases, but these were mainly behind the fold of the knee. Their shoes were neatly polished.

Charles Croaker was the physical education and sports teacher. He was bordering on morbidly obese, always dressed in an extra-large grey tracksuit and stained white plimsolls. The pupils had already nicknamed him: The Goliath Toad.

Drama and art were taught by Tobias Jubb. He was very entertaining and fun.

Arlo Spragg was deputy headmaster and taught maths and science. He was gifted at explaining both the processes and conclusions. However, he was quite eccentric and would often play a soft tune on his violin while a maths or science question was being processed. He was a former Spitfire pilot in World War II.

Victor Smudge was the history teacher. He had a very serious nature but was also very kind. Some pupils put his serious nature perhaps down to his wartime experience. He most enjoyed ancient history, as well as the Elizabethan and Georgian periods.

Finally, music, literature and English were taught by Montague Foxhall-Trott.

This teacher stood out by a country mile. Aged about thirty-five, he looked as if he'd just arrived from Eton College. His shoulder-length ash-blond hair was parted down the middle, and his dress was immaculate. He wore a crisp white shirt, with a penny round style detachable collar, supporting a silk paisley tie. His jacket was Harris Tweed with a silk handkerchief in the top pocket, while the sleeve length was just enough to show the shirt cuffs and silver cufflinks beneath. His fine-woven narrow grey slacks had a sharp crease down the centre, draped over well-polished brown Chukka boots. His mode of transport was a cream-coloured 1930s Rolls Royce Phantom, parked alongside his fellow teachers' bicycles and the headmaster's shiny green Morris Minor.

Tom greatly admired Mr Foxhall-Trott's flamboyant style of dress, his impeccable manners and charm.

CHAPTER 3
ALLOCATION OF PUPILS TO FORM MASTERS

In the assembly hall the pupils were lined up in rows and addressed by the deputy headteacher, Arlo Spragg.

He was of an average height and build with sandy-coloured wavy hair and a ruddy complexion. He sported a large handlebar moustache and was dressed in a thick-woven tweed suit with round leather patches on the elbows of the jacket. His shoes were of brown leather and neatly polished. His tie, worn over a crisp white shirt, was from his days as a Spitfire fighter pilot in World War II. It had diagonal stripes of maroon, white and dark navy with a peppering of silver wings to signify his pilot status. The whole outfit was covered with a black graduation gown from his university days.

In a loud, clear voice, Arlo Spragg stated: "You have all been given a sealed envelope when you entered the reception area. When I tell you—and not a moment before—you will open your envelope and read the contents inside.

"You may now open those envelopes in complete silence. Thank you.

"Behind you there are numbers marked between one and five. Please go and stand behind the numbers you have been allocated and wait for your form master to collect you and take you to your classroom."

Tom was holding number five.

The form masters came in single file. First was Charles Croaker, who marched off with group number one.

Next was Tobias Jubb, who took group two. Tom started to get very apprehensive about who was going to be his form master.

The next teacher to take a group of pupils was Arlo Spragg, group three.

The penultimate teacher was Victor Smudge, group four.

Tom was in the last group that had not been selected yet, but he was overjoyed, because he knew he would be in Montague Foxhall-Trott's class.

Montague Foxhall-Trott looked up at the sign displaying the number five and said, "Gentlemen, please follow me."

Tom could not contain himself. His pulse raced and his heart filled with joy; he could not have wished for a better Form Master. They all marched off to his classroom.

"Please find a seat once you have placed the articles you do not need on the coat rack at the rear of the classroom," Mr Foxhall-Trott told them, once they were there. "I will address you as Mister, followed by your surname. You will address me as sir. Now, in a clockwise manner, please stand up and give your name, followed by sir."

The pupils did so.

"Thank you, gentlemen, for that. In time, I will recall the face with the surname. An interesting range of surnames. Good—a cross-section of cultures, no doubt.

"Now you may open your everyday notepad and enter today's date. You will then clearly write in capital letters: 'PUNCTUALITY. GOOD MANNERS.'

"Gentlemen, these significant words have won and lost wars. However, in your case they could be the difference between getting that dream job or creating the wrong impression before you have even opened your mouth. Always arrive a minute or two before the time of your appointment. You should treat my lessons the same way, and practise good manners.

"For the moment all you need to know about me is that I was a former schoolmaster at one of the well-known public schools near Windsor. I will be responsible for teaching you three subjects: music, English language/literature and life skills. The other masters will teach you all the other remaining subjects.

"One thing I must stress very clearly at this stage. You are at all times representing Mr Montague Foxhall-Trott and your fellow pupils. I expect you to, and you will, stand out from the other pupils in this school.

"Remember a simple word: PRIDE. This can be achieved at no cost to you or your parents.

"You are required to always follow the dress code. Your school uniform will be free of marks or stains, even if all your leisure time is used in maintaining it. Shirts are to look crisp with the school necktie neatly tied in a Windsor knot. For those of you that may not know, the narrow end of the necktie has a diagonal seam. It is at this intersection you begin to form your knot. Using this guide, your necktie will finish at the correct length.

"A small white handkerchief is to be displayed no more than half an inch above the top pocket of your jacket. Pockets must be flat on both jacket and trousers. All you should be carrying about your person is a pen and notebook in your inside pocket and a well-pressed handkerchief in your trouser pocket.

"Your trousers are to have a sharp crease down the centre at all times. Black shoes are to be neatly polished throughout the day.

"Let us now start with one of our subjects: music. The school curriculum states than we have to learn some folk and traditional tunes and songs, and indeed, we will touch on those, but I wish to expose you to a wider range of music, including classical and world music. I take it that most of you may be familiar with a newspaper called *The New Musical Express*?"

Tom had a grin from ear to ear, and so did the other pupils.

"We will hold a weekly event by seeing which pupil can predict which artist or group will move up the singles chart by a certain number of places during the course of one week. We will concentrate on the top thirty only, because that's the number of pupils I have in my class. The winner will have the loan of my acoustic guitar with an instruction book on how to play it, for one week only.

"We will now turn to the subjects of English language and English literature. During this session you will learn grammar, how to compose a letter and complain effectively both orally and by letter. There will also be essays and short stories, both hand-written and oral, to improve composition and diction.

"Our final subject is life skills. This subject is not on the school curriculum, but I think it is essential to learn what is considered to be good manners and etiquette. Learning these skills will give you confidence, prestige and knowledge in the society around you.

"I have received the benefit of a public-school education due to the generosity of my parents, and I have taught at a public school. I believe you would be foolish to miss this opportunity. However, if you choose to instead run around the playground like a wildebeest for this half hour, it is your choice.

"This subject is voluntary and for those of you that wish to attend, it will be held in this room on a Tuesday at 12.30 sharp. Please bring your own notebook."

MUSIC

The popular music of the day mainly consisted of ballads and rock 'n' roll. The pupils were instructed to listen to both and identify the differences between the two.

Classical music was alien to both Tom and most of the pupils, but Foxhall-Trott created an atmosphere that made it addictive to listen to.

The blackout blinds, used during the last war, were drawn shut. Then a piece from one of the great composers was played within this darkened room. You could not hear a sound from the pupils; it was if they were transported into another world as the music played.

This introduction to classical music gave Tom and his fellow pupils a wonderful sensation. The pupils would then be asked to write down what the music meant to them. Tom could instantly see that music interpretation was different for each listener.

During one piece, Ravel's *Boléro*, Tom could see hordes of ancient warriors on horseback picking up the pace with the music as they rode towards their enemy.

ENGLISH LANGUAGE

Foxhall-Trott went quite deep into nouns, pronouns, verbs, adjectives, adverbs, prepositions, conjunctions and interjections, but these were all dealt with in such a manner that the pupils understood them by introducing a memorable story with each topic. Pupils were more than welcome to approach him after each lesson to discuss any part they did not fully understand.

There was also full participation on debating regarding who is for or against a motion. At no point was any voice to be raised in anger, and nobody was to speak when the speaker was at the lectern. Different debate topics were given by Foxhall-Trott on everyday subjects.

There were also many exercises on how to write a letter of complaint, ensuring the issue was contained in the first paragraph and the tone was cordial throughout.

Mock telephone conversations covering different situations in life were also acted out, followed by discussing the positive and negative points.

Tom was absolutely enthralled by all these lessons, soaking them up like a sponge.

LITERATURE

The curriculum dictated that works by Shakespeare, Chaucer, Defoe, Stevenson and du Maurier should be discussed. Other world authors, such as Hemingway, Twain, Poe and Melville, were just a few of those introduced over the coming years.

Foxhall-Trott's method of teaching these works to his pupils was to give an overview of the story and the characters, a WHO, WHERE and WHEN approach. This style of teaching was easily understood by Tom and the other pupils, making them fully understand the story by using key facts.

LIFE SKILLS

The first Tuesday lunchtime time arrived. At 12.30 sharp, the classroom door was opened.

"Please enter, gentlemen."

Tom was at the head of the queue and, to Foxhall-Trott's surprise, he was followed by eighteen other pupils. This figure grew to twenty-two within a few weeks, due to word of mouth within the class.

"Please use your notebooks as these lectures will not be repeated," Foxhall-Trott told the class. "New entrants will have to find someone who has made copious notes."

The following lectures were given over a period of multiple years, and periodic pauses were given during these half-hour lectures to ensure pupils were able to make adequate notes and sketches.

SOCIAL MEETING AND GREETING

"A firm handshake is important, but not a grip that would break bones, and definitely use a softer handshake when greeting a lady or small child. If you are not being introduced, offer your name and carefully listen to the other person's name. Repeat it mentally three times to remember it.

"Remember conversation starters such as: Have you travelled far? How do you know the host? What line of business are you in? And the weather, of course.

"If the awkward response is 'We've met before', say 'Your face looked familiar' and ask them what they are doing now. It may jog your memory.

"When you are speaking, stop immediately if the other person starts to speak. This is bad manners on the other person's behalf and they will soon identify their mistake if they keep repeating it.

"If you have invited someone to your home or an appointment, ensure that you are the one to greet them."

A CUP OF TEA

Foxhall-Trott had laid out a small table with a crisp white Irish linen cloth and placed on it a teapot, a milk jug, a cup and saucer with teaspoon, a sugar bowl with sugar lumps and sugar tongs, a tea strainer and finally a tea caddy.

"Black loose-leaf tea is the ingredient, gentlemen. Add the required portion for each guest into the warmed teapot, pour on boiling water and let it steep for about three to five minutes."

The pupils were carefully recording every word.

"The steeped tea should only be served by the host/hostess with the tea strainer placed over the cup. The strainer is returned to its receptacle on the table. Do not pour multiple cups at the same time. The guest should be asked if they prefer their tea weak or strong. To achieve weak tea, only fill half of the cup and top it up with hot water.

"Ask if milk, sugar or lemon are required. If no milk is required, only sugar and lemon, the guest should add the sugar first as the citric acid from the lemon will prevent the sugar from dissolving. The lemon slices should be placed on a decorative plate with a small fork for lifting the lemon to the saucer if required.

"If granulated sugar is being offered, the spoon in the sugar bowl *must not* be placed into the tea. Sugar lumps should be transferred by the tongs to the saucer and gently placed into the tea.

"A dry biscuit, if offered, should be placed on a side plate and broken in two before eating. *Never* dip a biscuit into your tea. While drinking your tea, you should only look straight ahead and place your index finger through the handle with your thumb on the top. Never put your hand around a cup.

"The saucer should be left on the table, and when you have finished your tea, place the cup handle and the stem of the spoon at four o'clock on the saucer."

Tom was absolutely enthralled by these weekly half-hour sessions put on by Foxhall-Trott. He felt that he was gaining access to a society steeped in tradition, order and good manners. Tom's family had to put up with his enthusiasm when he returned home from school every Tuesday.

CHAPTER 4
CHARLIE CROAKER

The remaining school lessons seemed rather dull to Tom, and one lesson in particular, which appeared twice a week: physical education and sport. Mainly because this was organised by Charlie Croaker, a morbidly obese bully.

Croaker could not carry out any gymnastic or sporting activity due to his obesity. He would always find a pupil to demonstrate what he wanted the pupils to do by repeatedly bullying them until they did what he wanted.

Periodic boxing match lessons were held in the assembly hall, which was also equipped as a gymnasium. Croaker enjoyed these sessions, sitting on his three-legged wooden stool like a fat Roman emperor watching gladiatorial games.

Each month, he would set up the boxing ring. Corner posts were slotted into the hall floor and the enclosure ropes attached to them. Padded mats were laid inside the ring. Croaker, as usual, would select the most mismatched pupils in height and build. The contest would not be ended until one or both pupils' faces were blooded. He would then bark, "GO AND GET SHOWERED."

CROAKER'S ATTEMPED REVENGE
None of the students would ever forget the session. Croaker was growling for more action. He rose from his stool and put on a pair of boxing gloves.

"You, Bennett!" he shouted. "Put those gloves on and get into the ring."

Alfie "Skinny" Bennett was about 5'9", exceptional for a fourteen-year-old, thin as a rake and very pale. Alfie had a quiet demeanour and mixed with a similar group of pupils.

A wide grin appeared on Tom's face, and the other boys'. Alfie was the county schoolboy boxing champion. Obviously, Croaker wasn't aware of this.

"Right, Bennett, put your defence up like this."

Alfie just kept touching Croaker's gloves.

"Come on, boy, try and break through my defence. Don't be a wimp."

Tom and his classmates came in closer to the ring ropes, determined not to miss what was about to unfold. Croaker was beating his chest like a silverback gorilla, barking, "Come on, Bennett! Try and break my defence."

Alfie immediately went into his attacking mode, his footwork and hand movements clearly taking Croaker by surprise. Alfie threw numerous punches into Croaker's fat stomach, to the approving roar of the class.

This assault immediately lowered Croaker's defence, exposing his upper body. Alfie wasted no time in exploiting this weakness. He quickly started attacking Croaker's jaw, sending his face left then right, repeating this using alternate fists.

Croaker's arms dropped to his side and his fat frame wobbled as he collapsed to his knees on the cushioned mat, shouting, "STOP! STOP!"

He could hardly be heard above the cheering of the class. Alfie quickly withdrew to his corner. Croaker turned and sat upright, resting against the corner post, panting and sweating. His eyes were still glazed over.

Just for a moment, Tom and his classmates had their elbows on the top ring rope, just staring at Croaker as though the beast had been slain. Then two pupils leapt into the ring to untie the laces on Alfie's gloves. Alfie, ever the professional, went over to his opponent to see if he was alright.

"GET OUT, ALL OF YOU, GET OUT!" shouted Croaker.

The class left the hall sporting the widest grins. Word of Alfie's boxing match spread around the school quicker than greased lightning.

The following morning, Foxhall-Trott asked Alfie to stand up.

"Mr Bennett, I understand you achieved a successful result in a sporting match yesterday against Mr Croaker."

"Yes, sir, I did."

"I could never understand the sport myself. In the animal kingdom, the males of the species usually fight to win the favours of a female to breed with—was that your intention, Bennett?"

"No, sir," Alfie replied with a crimson face.

"Good to hear, Mr Bennett. Anyway, an honourable success always deserves a round of applause. Gentlemen."

The class stood up and loudly clapped and cheered Alfie, who just stood there looking very embarrassed. He had quickly become the school hero.

"However, gentlemen," said Foxhall-Trott, "I have some disturbing news that I have to read out to you. It is from Mr Croaker.

"Dear Mr Foxhall-Trott,

"It is with great sadness that I must report that your entire class behaved disgracefully in one of my lessons, and as a result, I wish that they all assemble in the school hall after school and remain in detention with me in silence for one hour over a two-week period. If any pupil breaks that silence, the punishment will be repeated.

"Yours sincerely, Charles Croaker."

There were groans all around the classroom and comments of "That's not fair!" Tom had an after-school job working for Ginger on his vegetable market stall, and his immediate thoughts were the loss of half his wages from Ginger and the free bag of daily vegetables.

"Well, gentlemen, you have a decision to make. You have been taught how to handle situations similar to this, and I am confident that someone is going to tell me how."

The whole class in unison shouted, "Debate, sir! Debate!"

"Then I propose that I set up a meeting with the headmaster during a lunchtime for one of you to put your case forward as to why this detention should not be imposed. You will each write down on a piece of paper the name of the candidate you wish to represent you at this meeting, which I will also attend."

The folded pieces of paper were gathered on Foxhall-Trott's desk. He opened up each one and placed them into neat piles. The whole class could see that the three piles were distinctly different in size.

"Gentlemen, we have a clear winner with eighty-three per cent of the votes. Mr Larsen, please step forward. You have been selected to represent your class."

Applause came from everyone, even those who did not vote for Tom.

"Mr Larsen, you need to start thinking about your strategy regarding your opposition to this detention," Foxhall-Trott told Tom, then turned to the class. "Gentlemen, remember this well: in matters concerning debating, you will never lose. You will win, or you will learn from it."

While they were present together in the staffroom, Foxhall-Trott broached the subject of an office lunchtime meeting to discuss the boxing match lesson with Edwin Lombard-Stoat and Mr Croaker. Lombard-Stoat was clearly unhappy that such a matter required any attention at all. Croaker spoke only to say that he had more important things to do than discuss the rantings of schoolboys who cannot take their punishment.

"Mr Croaker, it may be in your interest to listen to what my pupils' representative has to say," Foxhall-Trott suggested. "We may all learn something."

Lombard-Stoat, though angry that a teacher had seen to encourage pupils to challenge the establishment, said, "Very well, Mr Foxhall-Trott, I will see you in my office with this representative at 12.30 sharp tomorrow."

"Please excuse me, headmaster," said Croaker, "but I will not be attending. My lunch has more value that this conversation. However, I will prepare a chronological account of the event, for your information."

The following lunchtime arrived. Foxhall-Trott knocked on the headmaster's office door with Tom by his side, clutching a few notes of paper.

"Enter," came a growl from the other side of the door.

Lombard-Stoat was crouched over his desk. His dark, sunken eyes and greased-back black hair made him look like a large spider waiting to pounce on its prey.

Foxhall-Trott introduced Tom. "This is Mr Larsen, sir. The class selected him as their representative."

"Sit, Mr Larsen," said Lombard-Stoat, with a forced smile. "I have read Mr Croaker's account of the event during the boxing lesson, and therefore I will summarise it from Mr Croaker's point of view. He maintains that while he was demonstrating various arm and foot movements to be used in boxing, he invited one of the pupils to put on a pair of boxing gloves and spar with him so that the other pupils could learn the art of boxing. However, while he was sparring with the pupil, he lost his footing, but the pupil continued to spar, causing him to fall. This incident encouraged the whole class to start jeering at him. That is why he has imposed this detention."

Lombard-Stoat put down Croaker's report. "Seems reasonable to me. Mr Larsen, what do you think about that?"

"Absolutely not, sir."

This remark made Lombard-Stoat sit bolt upright in his chair. He'd never had his authority challenged before.

"Sir, may I fill in the gaps that Mr Croaker has left out? But before that, may I say that I have been a privileged pupil of this school for four years and I am due to leave school at the end of this year to make my way in society. As you can see, I am displaying the school badge on my jacket pocket, which has the school motto: '*Per Exemplum*'. It is a code we try to follow throughout our school life and hopefully beyond.

"In my four years at this school, I have never witnessed Mr Croaker 'lead by example'. I have also never seen him personally demonstrate a gymnastic move or a sporting activity. He has always selected a pupil to try and demonstrate by repeatedly heavily scolding them until he thinks they have achieved what he wanted to show the class.

"Regarding the boxing event that resulted in this detention, Mr Croaker's approach to boxing lessons is to pick completely mismatched pupils in build and height and let them just slog it out until the first blood is drawn.

"During that afternoon, Mr Croaker put on a pair of boxing gloves and told Mr Bennett to do the same. Mr Croaker was beating his chest, goading Mr Bennett not to be a wimp. Mr Bennett, sir, is tall and very thin, with a rather awkward gait, but he did step into the ring, and we heard Mr Croaker shouting, 'Come on, Bennett, break my defence.'

"Mr Croaker, sir, was completely unaware that Mr Bennett is the county schoolboy boxing champion.

"As soon as Mr Bennett entered the ring, he completely changed his demeanour and took on an experienced boxer's position. While Mr Croaker was still beating his chest in a goading manner, Mr Bennett swiftly moved in, throwing accurate blows at Mr Croaker, who became completely confused and, due to his lack of skill in boxing, fell to the ground screaming 'Stop, stop.'

"Mr Bennett immediately went over to his assistance but was pushed away. The jeering that Mr Croaker refers to sir was cheering, not jeering. I have seen you on many occasions, sir, cheer on our pupils during sports days and events between other schools."

"Thank you, Mr Larsen," said Lombard-Stoat, when Tom was done. "I think we have heard enough from you. Please leave the room."

As Tom was leaving, Foxhall-Trott caught his sleeve. "Not a word to anyone," he told him.

The following morning Foxhall-Trott announced that the class's detention period was extinguished. This was followed by a round of applause.

"However, gentlemen," he said, "I am going to write an apology letter to Mr Croaker, which you will all sign. This matter is now finished."

The class's usual routine soon resumed. Tom, as usual, looked forward to the Tuesday lunchtime session with Foxhall-Trott's wicker basket.

CHAPTER 5
AFTERNOON TEA AND FINE DINING

"Gentlemen, let us now take part in one of Britain's favourite pastimes, both at home and in our colonies."

Foxhall-Trott retrieved a large wicker picnic basket from his study. In it, he had all the utensils, napkins and crockery needed to educate his pupils on how an afternoon tea should be laid out. The pupils sketched it when it was all set up.

"This is usually served at four o'clock, and guests should arrive at least ten minutes before, for seating arrangements. When seated at a table in a private home or in a tearoom, there should be at each place setting a knife or butter spreader on the right side of the plate and a fork on the left. The knife, if used, should always be placed with the blade facing the plate, and the fork prongs should face upwards. A teaspoon may be placed in the saucer holding the cup, or to the right of the knife. The napkin is placed on the left.

"When serving cake or soft pastries, a fork should be used, and a knife or a butter spreader for jam or cream. Each dish should have its own serving spoon. *Never* use your own utensils to dip into the jam or cream.

"When seated, the guest should place the napkin on their lap to catch any spills."

At this point Tom raised his hand and said, "Sir, is it ok to—"

"Mr Larsen, I believe the word you are looking for is 'acceptable'."

"Sorry, sir. Is it acceptable to tuck the napkin into your shirt or under your chin while eating?"

"Mr Larsen, a napkin should only be tucked into a shirt to apply pressure to a wound. Place it on your lap, Mr Larsen, on your lap.

"If you have to temporarily leave the table, place your napkin on the back of your chair or seat. In high-class establishments, the waiter will refold your napkin.

"I have no intention of repeating the making and serving of a cup of tea, as has been touched upon over the previous months and school terms. Look up your notes.

"Now let us look at the three-tiered plates, called the curate, that are set up for an afternoon tea. The top plate, being the first course, should hold the savones. These are savoury, finger-width sandwiches, preferably a mixture of different types of bread and fillings.

"The middle plate, or second course, should contain a mixture of plain and fruit scones. When you have selected which one you prefer, place it on your side plate and then cut the scone around the equator with your knife. You can choose to just add butter or have them Devon style by adding clotted cream first with a topping of strawberry jam, or Cornish style by adding jam first, followed with the cream topping. To remember which style is which, if you are being served a scone: Cornwall begins with the letter 'C', gentlemen, for cream on top.

"Gentlemen, remember the spoons in both the jam dish and clotted cream dish are used to take the ingredients to the scone. Never put your own utensil in those dishes.

"The bottom plate, the last course, is for small pastries. If some pastries are soft or cream filled, then your pastry fork should be used to eat them. Use your side plate knife to cut other pastries into bitesize pieces."

Mr Foxhall-Trott, turning to his pupils, said, "These lunchtime lectures on tea and afternoon tea should now put you at ease when attending such functions. If you have any queries or questions on what you have learned so far, speak out now."

The queries raised were merely indicative of the pupils' lack of concentration, and were dismissed with a suggestion made to retrieve the information from other pupils who had paid attention.

"Our next series of lectures will be related to the topic of dining, so I suggest that you sharpen your pencils and sleep well before attending, because in society, gentlemen, it is at these functions people will judge your breeding."

DINING

This lecture began with the now-familiar sight of Foxhall-Trott carrying his large wicker picnic basket, which he laid on the table.

Tom always looked forward to these lunchtime lectures and could not wait to demonstrate to his grandfather and aunt what he had learnt from each lecture.

"Tom is becoming very posh now, Grandad," his aunt said. "Showing us all these fancy ways the toffs use."

"I think it's a good idea," replied Grandad. "At least he won't feel embarrassed like we and the other guests were when attending the rare wedding breakfast, sat like fools, waiting for the waiter to show us which utensil to pick up."

Tom's face had immediately lit up; his expression indicated something was turning over in his brain. Perhaps all the life skills Foxhall-Trott was teaching them could be turned into a business.

"Gentlemen," said Foxhall-Trott, "I will start with two very important points:

"The only joint that should be on the dining table is the meat. NO HANDS OR ELBOWS.

"When being served, do not bob about on your seat like a bottle cork on the water. Sit upright and look straight ahead, because you will be served from your left and used crockery will be removed from your right-hand side.

"I will explain each item and its position on the table as we move along. I request that you carefully sketch these items, their location, and note what they are used for.

"The dinner plate (rarely referred to as the charger) should be in the centre of the setting. That is where the guest will be seated. A dinner fork with the prongs upright should be laid to the left-hand side of the plate, with the salad fork (if required) next to that. Dinner knife to the right, with the blade facing the plate, and the soup spoon next to that, with the spoon stem facing towards the table edge. If on the menu, the small shellfish fork should be set alongside the soup spoon. The base of all these utensils should line up with the base of the dinner plate.

"I think Gentlemen, we will leave the lecture at this point to give you time to sketch the utensils' locations and descriptions. I would suggest that enough room is left at the top of your notepad to include what is placed above the dinner plate."

Tom carefully noted every object laid out and carefully labelled them all. These lectures gave Tom so much confidence in knowing how to exercise manners if he ever attended any of these functions.

His grandad and aunt would be put through all these lectures, watching Tom lay out the table with the limited utensils and crockery in the household. Tom would demonstrate, saying, "Imagine this was a smaller fork, then it would be placed here next to the soup spoon, for shellfish."

Grandad and his aunt would be smiling and nodding in support of the knowledge he was gaining.

"Well done, Tom," commented Grandad.

Over the next few lectures, Foxhall-Trott moved on to what was placed above the dinner plate.

"A dessert fork and spoon are placed with the fork facing right with its prongs upright and the spoon bowl upright towards the left.

"The table napkin is generally folded and placed on the small side plate. This plate holds the butter knife and the folded napkin. Napkins folded in the shape of a pyramid should only be left on the plate if they are made of stone. If a salad and soup are being served, then a small salad plate is placed on the dinner plate with the soup bowl on top.

DRINKING GLASSES

"Glasses used for the meal should be positioned at one o'clock to the dinner plate. Working from left to right, you should have the glass for water, next to that should be the glass for red wine, and next to that the white wine glass. Below the white wine glass, you position the champagne flute.

"Gentlemen, it will be at least another four years, at the age of eighteen, before you are allowed to drink alcohol in this country. However, seeing that we are talking about the subject: red wine is normally served at room temperature, white wine and champagne are both served chilled—but not too chilled as they can lose some of their flavour.

"Always hold the glass by its stem so that you do not alter the temperature of the drink contained within the glass. While dining, never lift a glass while using your utensil; always rest your utensils on the dinner plate at four o'clock and eight o'clock respectively.

"If you ever invite guests to a meal at your home or a venue, make sure you are the person to greet them and offer them a drink upon arrival."

"I trust that your notes and sketches are all up to date, as there will be no repeat. Shall we now move on to how to use the utensils around your dinner plate?"

UTENSIL USAGE AND GOOD MANNERS

"This lecture, gentlemen, is as important as the Judgement of Solomon. The way you command yourself at the dining table is an open book as to your breeding.

"You should start in the order of the furthest from the dinner plate and work inwards. A salad fork is placed on the extreme left and a seafood fork on the extreme right, both with their prongs facing upwards. Both of these utensils should be used individually (for the dish served) in the hand you normally use to write with.

"The soup spoon is between the seafood fork and dinner knife. Keep the soup bowl on the table, never lift or tilt it. Do not place the stem of the spoon in the palm of your hand, but rest it between your thumb and index finger.

"Any surplus soup on the spoon should be removed by moving it across the lip of the soup bowl. Take the soup from the centre of the bowl and sip the soup. Do not make a slurping noise.

"The bread roll on the side plate should have a bitesize piece broken off it, and the butter you should have placed on the rim of the plate, to be applied with the butter knife to that piece of bread roll.

"The dinner knife is held in the hand you normally write with, holding the base of the handle in your central palm and your index finger on the back edge of the knife blade to apply pressure when cutting food. The same principle is applied when using your fork. If your host unfortunately serves peas with the meal, give that dish a miss. If you accept, press the peas into the back of the fork prongs. Do not be tempted to scoop them up on the fork.

"If you are ever invited to a dinner and the utensils are of silverware, please remember that when you have finished your meal, the prongs of the fork are placed down on the plate. This is to avoid the possibility of too much silverware being immersed in the jus or gravy, which may be acidic."

CHAPTER 6
ARLO SPRAGG

Arlo Spragg was the maths and science teacher who made learning fun. His portly figure, ruddy complexion and handlebar moustache stood out anywhere within the school grounds. He sometimes had the habit of gently playing his violin while pupils solved his set problem.

During World War II, he'd been a pilot, flying Spitfires. This experience seemed to have made him a very contented person who believed in the concept of "Carpe Diem". Pupils would often distract him when his questions related to physics such as linear collisions and other puzzles by making him bring aircraft into the explanation.

He would ramble back to his days as a wartime pilot. "When Fritz..." he would say, taking a stick of chalk and walking over to the blackboard. There was never any malice in his voice; he accepted that both sides had been serving their country. His diagram of Fritz's aeroplane and his own during a dogfight would demonstrate the stresses and strain put on both the wings and the fuselage of the aeroplanes, considering speed and direction. He would even demonstrate the most critical location on the aeroplane if a bird collided into it, both the angle and speed of the impact could have dire consequences. His short stories would clearly explain the solution to the problem and many others. The pupils would copy this information into their notebooks.

Even though many of the academic lessons were interesting to listen to, Tom always looked forward to his Tuesday lunchtime lectures with Foxhall-Trott the most.

TOM'S PART-TIME JOBS
Tom lived in a community where marriages, christenings and funerals were continuous throughout the year, and despite this area being considered poor and working class, there was always

a quiet rivalry between families to try and go one step better than the previously held function. Tom could see an opening to earn money from this foolish rivalry.

He was also aware of a Jewish community less than a quarter of a mile away from the enclave he lived in, who also held ceremonial functions.

To start his business Tom would require all the accessories Mr Foxhall-Trott used during his Tuesday lunchtime lectures. He visited many second-hand shops within the City to gauge how much money he would need to purchase these items, as well as a small hand truck to carry his accessories to venues.

THE CITY OPEN-AIR MARKET STALLS

A part-time job that Tom had held since the age of eleven was assisting on a vegetable stall for ten shillings per week plus a bag of vegetables for each day he attended.

After school until 5.30 p.m. and all day Saturday, Tom's job was to ensure the front of the stall was always well stocked. The stallholder, Albert "Ginger" Reynolds, and his full-time assistant, Sammy Biggs, maximised the profits by accepting stock from the fruit and veg wholesalers that was not as fresh as it could be, usually a week or so past its best.

Saturday morning was a busy time for Tom. He would meet Ginger outside the wholesalers at 6 a.m. and wait at the entrance while Ginger did his usual negotiating. The wholesaler would loan them their large four-wheel cart to pull the produce to the market stall, approximately two hundred yards away.

While Ginger and Sammy were setting up the stall, Tom would get started on trimming the yellow leaves on the cabbages and cauliflowers. Carrots that had started to go rubbery were thrown away. Tom would bring the trimmed vegetables around to the front of the stall and start laying the produce out in an attractive pattern.

Ginger was not well educated but he was streetwise and had a wonderful patter with his customers. As he was serving a customer, he would say, "Look, she don't wear glasses, she has been buying my carrots for years." He would always throw a few extra potatoes or sprouts into an elderly customer's bag, saying something funny about their frown or their type of clothing. His customers loved this banter and would often interact with him, making his showmanship even funnier. Sammy would act as his straight man.

During the lunchtime hours the stall would never close, so Ginger would take money from the till and send Tom to a market stall serving hot drinks, sandwiches, pies and hot snacks. Tom would take the "billy can" (an enamel jug with an attached cup) for the tea and buy three hot steak and kidney pies. "Tell Harry they are for Ginger!" he would always shout, to get the stallholders' discount.

Tom gave some of his weekly earnings to the household and put away the rest in a Post Office Savings book. His objective now was to start up his new business venture.

TOM'S NEW BUSINESS VENTURE

Tom's first purchase from a second-hand shop was a large, well-made wicker picnic basket. He ensured that all the inset pockets and leather straps were in good condition to hold the crockery in place when transporting it around. A smaller wicker basket was to hold his high tea service set.

His most difficult task was to find a set of matching dinner-ware and a high tea set for one person. They had to be of the finest bone china.

The second-hand dealers became quite used to seeing Tom pop into their shops looking for various items to stock his baskets. Some of them would say, "Tom, I thought this may be of interest to you," and show him a specific item they'd found. If Tom liked it, he would show slight interest but then walk away, looking at other items. He was mimicking what Ginger would do when getting the best bargain. He would say, "It's not exactly what I'm looking for, but maybe I could use it for something."

Over a period of months, Tom stocked his wicker picnic baskets. To ensure he had everything he needed to start his business venture, he laid out the contents of the baskets on the table at home.

First, he laid out a freshly pressed Irish linen tablecloth supplied by his aunt as a gift to start his business. His grandad and aunt looked on with wide smiles as Tom carefully arranged all the dinnerware, utensils and glasses, exactly as Foxhall-Trott had shown him. Tom would occasionally refer to his school notebook just to reassure himself that the arrangement was perfect.

Tom gently closed the dining room door while he practised his commentary on how you should lay everything out and what each item was used for. During his visits to various second-hand shops, he had purchased (for a few pennies) a selection of menu cards with their holders from former high-class hotels and cafés.

This gave his clients an idea of what utensils to use related to the menu card selected. These menus had the best of British fare, and some had no pork or shellfish products displayed, because Tom also had an eye on hopefully introducing his etiquette lectures to the nearby Jewish community.

MARKETING

Tom purchased a pack of blank postcards and proceeded to write on them in capital letters:

NEVER BE EMBARRASSED AGAIN ABOUT WHICH UTENSIL TO USE AT A WEDDING, BANQUET OR AFTERNOON HIGH TEA.

CONTACT: MR TOFF'S ETIQUETTE SERVICES, 7 ASPECT PLACE, SUMMERTON.

His postcards were placed into shop windows within the locality for sixpence per week. Some shops offered a month's display for ninepence.

CHAPTER 7
JACOB'S CAFÉ

A certain street within the City had several Jewish businesses, such as a bakery, outfitters, jewellers, delicatessens, shoemakers and butchers. The focal point for this community was Jacob's Café. It was always full, particularly on a Sunday after the Sabbath.

The owners, a husband and wife, were a warm-hearted, middle-aged, childless Jewish couple, Lionel and Miriam Jacob. They were both of Polish origin, and you would never see one without the other.

Lionel was quite tall and slim with black hair, round brown eyes and a fresh complexion. He sported a thin black moustache above a wide smile, exposing white teeth that had a small gap between the front two. His daily attire was a white shirt and black tie beneath a light brown overall coat. A notebook and pen were always visible within his top pocket.

Miriam was short and wide with curly, short dark-brown hair, clipped on both sides with decorative hair slides. Her beautiful green eyes and bright smile lit up a plump olive-skinned face. Her floral duster coat partly covered a plain white blouse and tweed skirt, while she floated around the café on kitten-heeled brown shoes.

Lionel and Miriam were assisted by two young Eastern European refugee girls that seemed to look upon the owners as their parents. The love and respect flowed both ways. The girls dressed in black uniforms with white pinafore aprons and tiara caps in the 1920s style. A large sign in the kitchen, adjacent to the door into the dining area, said 'SMILE'.

The café frontage had two plain glazed panels either side of a central door. The interior tried to bring a touch of class with a crystal chandelier at each end of the room. The wood panel finishes to the walls were of light oak, with large black-and-white photographs of European capital cities to remind patrons of home.

Tables and chairs were arranged in settings of twos and fours but could easily be rearranged to accommodate larger groups. To one side of the café was the display counter showing a variety of pastries, such as honey and apple cake, baked in different ways with flavoured fillings and toppings. The specialty breads and bagels were placed in wicker baskets both in front of the counter and behind. A large blackboard placed high behind the counter showed the day's fare. This changed on Monday and Wednesday.

During the summer a selection of salads were offered and there were always two types of soup. Chicken soup never went off the menu. Other hearty dishes such as kasha with varnishkes latkes, carrot tzimmes flavoured with ginger, and sweet noodle kugel. The smell of hot brewed coffee and lemon tea always filled the air.

Lionel would go from table to table ensuring his guests had everything they needed. Miriam was the powerhouse of the café; she commanded the whole show. The customers chattering in different mother tongues made the café sound more like a happy children's playground.

Tom was on a nodding acquaintance with Lionel and Miriam from visiting their café on Sundays to buy bread. Most shops were closed on a Sunday under the Shops Act 1950, but Jewish-owned shops could open from 2 p.m. They had to close on Saturdays instead.

Miriam would call to Lionel, "Lionel, Bruchale (*little blessing*) is here!" Tom would try to get a loaf similar to British white or brown bread. Sometimes all that was left for sale was challah. They had to keep certain types of bread for their customer orders.

On one of these Sunday afternoon visits, Tom mentioned his business venture to Lionel and asked about displaying one of his postcards in their café.

"Bruchale, we are very busy right now, but call back at six o'clock tomorrow," Lionel told him.

The café closed at 5.30 on Mondays but Tom had his nose pressed against the glass panel in the entrance door at 6 o'clock sharp.

Lionel came to the door and welcomed him in. Miriam came from the kitchen area, wiping her hands in a tea towel.

"Sit," she said to Tom. "What is this new business of yours?"

Tom outlined his business proposal and showed them the postcard he would like to display in their café.

"Oy vey," shouted Miriam, "the name is all wrong, Bruchale! We are not a British café," she said, looking at Tom's details. "We like your business idea and we think there could be a need for it with some of our customers. Weddings, bar mitzvahs and posh teas, but it is not something we will use here."

Lionel and Miriam asked Tom to bring his wicker baskets to the café after closing time that Wednesday evening.

Tom arrived promptly on Wednesday evening and started to set out both his afternoon tea and dinner settings on the café tables while Lionel and Miriam were preparing the other tables for the next day.

"First," said Miriam, "if we like it, we will display your cards around the café, but on the bottom put: ASK LIONEL OR MIRIAM, ABRAMOWIZC ETIQUETTE SERVICES."

Tom was confused about the name Abramowizc Etiquette Services and asked what it meant.

"We are not stealing your business, Bruchale," said Miriam. "That is my maiden name before I was married and I have always wanted it to be displayed somewhere in our café."

Tom laughed and said the spelling looked better than Larsen.

Over the previous weeks Tom had revised and memorised his presentation word for word, explaining clearly each piece of utensil and crockery and the manner in how and when to use them.

"I am going to remove this small fork on the extreme right-hand side," he explained.

"Why?" said Miriam.

"Because it is used for a shellfish dish and I do not want to offend a client's religion."

Tom went through the whole range of table manners, showing how the utensils should be laid on the plate when lifting a glass, pointing out that all these manners were very important because they signalled to the waiter/server at what stage you were at with that course.

While his presentation was going on, the café owners were looking at Tom with knowing smiles of appreciation at how professional he was.

"You are a clever boy, Bruchale, and you have clearly done your homework," said Miriam.

Lionel and Miriam were childless and had taken a shine to him.

"We love it, Bruchale. We have been in this business a long time and we see a lot of things in what you have shown us that we can improve and would not cost anything. We will not be serving any of the type of fancy settings you have displayed, but little things like how a cup, saucer and spoon should be displayed look so nice and professional. We like you and your business venture, so this is what we propose:

"We have a customer, Mauri Goldstein, who is a printer and he prints anything we need for the café. We suggest that the cards should read:

"SHALOM, NEVER BE EMBARRASSED AGAIN ABOUT WHICH UTENSIL TO USE AT A WEDDING, BANQUET OR AFTERNOON HIGH TEA. ASK LIONEL OR MIRIAM ABOUT ABRAMOWIZC ETIQUETTE SERVICES.

"Now, Bruchale, how much are you going to charge for these services?"

Tom had already thought this out. "For the experience at a wedding, bar/bat mitzvah or special dining event it will be ten shillings for four guests and an additional two shillings and sixpence per additional guest. My thinking behind this is at a wedding the four could be the bride, the groom and the bride's parents, but I assume that the groom's parents will not want to be left out looking uneducated at the top table; therefore, that's fifteen shillings earned.

"A bar/bat mitzvah could operate in the same way, except the privileged boy or girl's tuition is free as a gift, provided they bring their parents or grandparents.

"The high tea experience will be five shillings for two and two shillings and sixpence for each extra guest, assuming four will wish to share the table for such an event."

"You seem to have thought this through, Bruchale," said Miriam. "So, business is business. To display your cards in the café, we will want ten per cent on every successful referral we pass onto you. How do you feel about that?"

"Well," said Tom, "this could raise the profile of your café." They both nodded and smiled. "But I think it is fair, provided that for every third successful referral I can have a free coffee and a toasted bagel with honey."

"Bruchale, you will make a good businessman. It's a deal. We will place the printed cards around the café as discussed. If anybody is interested, we will take their name. Come to the café every two days to see if we have any interest."

Tom thought it was only fair to tell Ginger about his idea to start up a business while still at school. To Tom's surprise, Ginger was one hundred per cent behind him, briefly telling him how he'd started his own business.

"You are hardworking, honest and reliable," said Ginger. "I'm sure you will make a success of it. Let's see how it goes and if you are unable to make a shift at the stall I will rely on you to provide another boy like you on the same money."

"Absolutely, Ginger," said Tom, relieved that it had all gone so well.

CHAPTER 8
FOXHALL-TROTT'S LEGACY

Tom thought that now would be a good time to tell Foxhall-Trott about his proposed business.

At the end of the school day, Tom asked Mr Foxhall-Trott if he could have a word with him.

"Step into my anteroom, Mr Larsen," said Foxhall-Trott. "What seems to be bothering you?"

"Oh, nothing, sir. You are always encouraging us to think of business ventures to make our way in the world when we leave school, which will be next year."

"Correct, Mr Larsen. So?"

Tom told him about his part-time job on the market stall which had provided some income and free vegetables. It had taught him about hard work, honesty, reliability and how to deal with members of the public, but it offered no future.

"To own your own stall, or a few, could offer you a good future, Mr Larsen."

"Yes, sir, but your Tuesday lunchtime lectures have given me the drive to seek more out of life. They have given me so much confidence."

"Good," said Foxhall-Trott. "Now, what did you want to discuss?"

Tom told him all about his new business venture, and the deal he'd made with Lionel and Miriam.

"What I am really asking, sir, is do I have your permission to use the knowledge I gained from your lectures to try and make this a business?"

"Mr Larsen, my lectures were titled 'Life Skills', and I am pleased to learn that at least one pupil had been listening and taking notes. The whole idea of these lectures was to educate and better oneself. You have clearly taken that view. I wish you every success in your business and I would appreciate if you would give me a periodic update on your progress.

"May I ask one thing of you, Mr Larsen? Whatever the outcome of your business, you will give your word as a gentleman that you will pass on your skills to the disadvantaged and underprivileged where possible. Education can open many doors. It was a pledge my father asked me to make at a young age, when I went off to boarding school."

"With pleasure, sir, and thank you for your time.

"Pleasure, Mr Larsen, pleasure."

AWAITING REFERRALS

Several weeks passed, and Tom had not received any names of people that may be interested in his presentations. Every other day, as agreed with Lionel and Miriam, Tom would call into the café after his duties with Ginger, clutching his free bag of vegetables. The café owners would only shrug.

Tom was undaunted; he had total confidence that there was a market for his services. Finally, during one evening while the family were listening to the radio, there was a knock on the door. Tom's aunt Anja answered it.

"Tom!" she called. "It's somebody for you."

A tall man was at the door, almost filling the door frame.

"Is your father, Tom Larsen, there?" he asked Tom.

"No, sir. My parents passed away several years ago due to the influenza pandemic."

The man took a step back and apologised. "I'm very sorry to hear that, I just assumed that I would be talking with an adult about the services being offered, not a schoolboy."

"Well, you have come to the right place. My name is Tom, and yours?"

"Mr Rafferty."

"Please come in, Mr Rafferty."

Tom led him into the parlour.

Tom's home was set within an enclave of approximately three hundred terraced houses, built during the 1850s to house workers to construct the nearby docks, factories and warehouses. These industries created a multi-cultural society.

They were two storeys high, having a slate-covered roof, stone-faced walls and multi-paned glass windows set into painted wooden sash windows. The front door was of solid timber with a brass letterbox, door knocker and house number, plus an iron handle to pull it shut.

To keep the property secure, a substantial lock was fixed to the interior of the door. The painted woodwork was of different colours to denote which landlord owned which property, as all these properties were rented. The houses were set out in a series of streets and courtyards and were all set directly off the outside footway.

The interior was simple. Three bedrooms on the first floor were accessed via a steep wooden staircase. The ground floor contained a kitchen with a cold-water supply, a living room and a front parlour used for special days or guests.

Heating was provided by cast-iron open fireplaces. The ground floor ones had a central section for the burning of fuel and oven sections to the side for cooking and warming food. The upper bedrooms also had small open fireplaces to warm the upper floor during the winter months.

Each side of the chimney breasts had gaslight fittings, still in working order, although the houses had been modernised with a limited amount of electric lighting and power sockets. The gas and electrical supply both worked off a penny-coin operated payment meter.

The rear gardens were narrow with a central path beneath rope clothes lines. The boundary walls were of random rubble stonework about four foot high and usually painted in a lime wash that helped reflect some light during the nighttime when visiting the outside privy. Toilet paper consisted of old newspapers.

In the parlour, Mr Rafferty was asked to take a seat. Tom had already planned out in his mind where potential customers would sit if they ever called to discuss his services. Over the fireplace mantelpiece were photographs of current and past members of Tom's family, either side of a marble-encased carriage clock.

Within the fireplace surrounds stood a brass fender, tongs and iron poker, all next to a coal bucket. The fireplace remained unlit.

A small sign strategically placed behind Tom's chair read: "'The man who asks a question is a fool for a minute, the man who does not ask is a fool for a lifetime.' Confucius, 551 B.C." Tom had never forgotten those words Miss Amelia Pratt mentioned to him in junior school.

Tom saw Mr Rafferty peering over his shoulder, reading the sign.

"How can I help?" asked Tom.

"Well, I saw the postcard in Stav Caperos's shop window and it made me think about the experience I had at my eldest daughter's wedding. The caterers I booked were fine. When we arrived, the tables were all laid out professionally, to my daughter and son-in law's delight.

"Unfortunately, the only catering staff left behind the scenes were the chef and servers to bring out the various courses of the meal. We were obviously on the top table and completely ignorant about what utensil to use in what order when the food was arriving. I have never felt so embarrassed in my life, and the guests were also confused and looking at us for some guidance. I want a situation where we look in control and the guests are following the lead of the top table."

"Mr Rafferty," said Tom, "I specialise in guiding clients through all the correct etiquette on such occasions, and I would be more than happy to help you."

With that, Tom brought the larger of the two wicker baskets into the parlour and opened it up. "In here, Mr Rafferty, I have all the crockery, utensils and glasses you would wish to find at any fine-dining experience. I will lay everything out in the order and position they are meant to be at a sitting for one person. I will explain what to use first and when to use it.

"My fee also includes showing you the correct manners to use while dining, such as where your napkin should be placed and the position of your utensils when pausing to drink from your glass. These are important signals to the servers to show if you have finished your course or not.

"I have written down my fee structure. Let me know if you are interested and I can then tell you what dates I have available to go through the whole sequence of events for whichever type of dining occasion you are interested in."

Tom acted as though these demonstrations were second nature to him.

"I would suggest that relatives such as your wife, daughter and future son-in-law meet at your home. Perhaps your future-in-laws would also like to attend, although I prefer not to demonstrate to more than eight people at a time."

"Tom, you came across as being very professional and I will be in touch," said Mr Rafferty.

Tom showed Mr Rafferty out, then he punched the air, whispering, "Yes!"

TOM'S FIRST COMMISSION

Communication at this time was generally by letter if there was some distance involved, as telephones were generally used for businesses, although some middle-class people and most of the upper-class had telephones. If working-class people wished to use a telephone, red telephone boxes were placed in various locations with a coin-operated system.

Within a day or two Mr Rafferty was at Tom's door again. He told Tom that his daughter was getting married in two weeks' time and that all the preparations had been made. The question was, when could Tom visit his home to give his presentation to the family members that would be sitting at the top table.

"I looked at your fee for eight people and I have worked the cost out to £1 exactly. Do you agree?"

"Absolutely," said Tom.

Mr Rafferty stretched out his hand, large compared to Tom's, to agree the deal. The deal was struck.

TOM'S PRESENTATION AT THE RAFFERTYS' HOME

Tom continued with his part-time market stall job after school, but as soon as he had eaten his evening meal, he would retire to the parlour to practise has presentation over and over again. His grandad and aunt had nothing but admiration for his dedication to making sure he provided a professional service.

The day arrived for his presentation at Mr Rafferty's home. Fortunately, this was located within a short walking distance from Tom's home. Grandad gave Tom a hand to place the wicker basket onto the sack truck, and Tom pushed it around to the venue. He paused for a moment outside the house and took a deep breath.

The brass door knocker was lifted and gently tapped against its plate. Mr Rafferty opened the door wide, greeting Tom with a smile. "Come on in, Tom, and meet the family."

The narrow hallway was filled with inquisitive faces. Tom could hear mutterings of "It's a schoolboy, he looks too young."

He lifted his sack truck with the wicker basket into the hall and asked Mr Rafferty where he would like him to set up the place setting.

"In the parlour would be fine."

Tom asked for a few minutes to set it up and then called in the family. The setting literally took about four minutes, as Tom had practised this so many times at home.

Tom stood facing the setting from the opposite side so that the place setting was in clear view of the guests. He'd brought along a thin bamboo stick to use as a pointer when giving out information.

Mr Rafferty quickly introduced Tom to the others; this included his wife, his daughter and her future husband, his parents, and the best man and his wife. They just smiled and nodded to Tom.

Pointing to the item in the order of their use, Tom spoke in a clear voice, then asked, after the explanation, if anybody had any questions. Nobody uttered a word. Tom wanted to encourage engagement with his guests. To do that he invented a scenario, saying that somebody had asked him these questions during another presentation; this helped to open up a conversation.

Tom was watching closely the expression on the guests' faces throughout the presentation, and it was so encouraging to hear the odd comment: "Well, I never knew that before."

After demonstrating the use and purpose of all the crockery and utensils set out, Tom again announced, "Are there any questions?"

Mr Rafferty was the first to speak. "Tom, I think I speak for everybody here—that was an excellent presentation and we have all learnt a lot about dining."

With that, the whole party clapped, their applause accompanied by various pleasing comments and congratulations.

"Now," said Tom, "my agreement with Mr Rafferty was also to show you the correct etiquette while you are at the dining table."

The guests looked both surprised and pleased that there was more to come. Tom demonstrated this next topic by sitting at the table and asking his captive audience to come around to the other side of the table so that Tom and the place setting were facing them.

While sitting in the chair, Tom picked up the table napkin and demonstrated that it was to be placed over the knees to catch any food. He took this opportunity to use one of Foxhall-Trott's expressions: "Never inside the blouse or shirt, only if it is to apply pressure to a wound." They laughed, the message hit home.

"Your napkin also acts as a signal to your server of what you intend on doing. If you leave the table for a comfort break…"

Mr Rafferty (remembering the Confucius sign in Tom's parlour), asked Tom, "What's a comfort break?"

"It is when you must leave the table to visit the toilet or maybe just to speak to another person in another area of the room."

The others were smiling, grateful that Mr Rafferty had asked the question in their inquisitive minds.

"If this happens," Tom continued, "place your napkin on the seat or back of your chair. This signifies to the server that you are just taking a break from the dining table. High-class restaurants will refold your napkin by the time you return.

"Now, let us move on to the food courses. As you can see, I am sat upright in my seat and that is the position you should hold when you see the server approaching your table. You will be served food from your left-hand side, and used crockery will be removed from your right-hand side. Therefore, there is no need to bob from one side to the other like a strolling penguin. I am sure you have seen this happen many times on these occasions."

Everybody was smiling and nodding in agreement.

"I previously explained the order in which the utensils are used, now a word about holding them. The shellfish and salad fork should be placed in the hand you write with and held by their stem handle when in use.

"This applies also to the soup spoon. Please remember that the soup is taken from the centre of the bowl, not from the edges, and do not tilt the bowl upwards or away from you to extract every dreg of soup. This is bad manners. The used forks and spoon should always be positioned at four o'clock on the crockery. This also applies to the dessert spoon and fork. The fork is always in your writing hand.

"If the table setting is correct, the blade of the knife should face the plate and the prongs on the fork should face upwards. If they have not been set out correctly, adjust them yourself—do not make a fuss. Have a quiet word later with the catering manager. He will appreciate this.

"Hold the knife in the hand you write with, with the stem in the palm of your hand. Remember, the knife and fork are not drumsticks. Use your index finger"—Tom flicked this finger back and forth—"to press down on the back edge of your knife to cut the food. The fork prongs should always face downwards on the plate and you either push food onto the back of the fork or prick into it to lift it. Never turn the fork over to use like a shovel. Push peas onto the back of the fork, do not scoop them up.

"While eating, take pauses while chewing your food and rest your knife and fork at four and eight o'clock, like this. Follow this practice when lifting a glass to take a drink. This utensil position also signals to the server that you have not finished, if you have to leave your seat.

"A word about wines at the table. Although I'm below the age to drink alcohol, as you can see"—the group smiled at that—"I have been shown the correct manners on this subject.

"Sparkling wines are served chilled, so hold the glass by its stem like this, so that you do not alter the wine's temperature. Red wines are served at room temperature, but I still recommend holding by the glass stem.

"Well, that's all I have to say about the subject of dining; I hope it has been helpful. Are there any questions?"

Again, his captive audience clapped and uttered words of praise. Mr Rafferty's chest was pushed outwards, knowing that what had been displayed was excellent and had impressed his family and future in-laws.

While the guests retired to the other room, Tom started to pack away his crockery, glasses and utensils into the wicker basket. Mr Raffety popped his head around the door and took some money out of his pocket.

"This is for you Tom, for a job well done."

Into Tom's hand was placed a one-pound note.

"That is what we agreed?" Mr Raffety asked.

"Yes, thank you," said Tom.

"Here is another ten-shilling note. We all chipped in because your presentation was well worth it. We have all learnt so much, and I doubt if we'll be embarrassed again."

Tom looked at the money he had received for just over an hour's work. His immediate thoughts were that it would take him three weeks working for Ginger to earn that sort of money.

Tom was in a hurry to get home and break the news to his grandfather and aunt on how the presentation went and, more importantly, the money he'd received.

One pound went straight into the household funds, despite Grandad and Aunt Anja pleading with Tom that he earned it and he should keep it. Tom would have none of it, saying if it were not for them, he would be in an orphanage.

CHAPTER 9
BACK IN THE CLASSROOM

Tom continued with his schoolwork with Foxhall-Trott but he did not reveal to any of his classmates his new business venture. He was fully aware that many of his fellow pupils had also been tutored during Foxhall-Trott's lunchtime lectures, and stayed silent so as to avoid any classmate rivals.

Tom followed his daily routine of working for Ginger after school and accepting his free bag of mixed vegetables followed by his weekly payment of ten shillings after his full Saturday shift. He was still calling into Jacob's Café every other day after his duties with Ginger.

Tom made his periodic visit to see Lionel and Miriam. He walked in with a wide smile. "I have some news for you both. I carried out my first presentation, and they were so pleased they paid me fifty per cent more."

"Bruchale, this is wonderful," said Miriam. "Well, we have some good news for you also. Saul and Davina Rosen have a fiftieth wedding anniversary in three weeks, and they are holding it in the banqueting room of the city hall. They want you to meet them here this Sunday afternoon to discuss your fees and the services you offer."

When Tom walked into the hallway at home, his aunt came from the kitchen area at the rear.

"Tom, your meal has been kept warm in the oven. Eat it quick as you can because Mr Rafferty called earlier today to find out what time you would be home. I told him about six thirty this evening, so you have half an hour to eat your meal."

Tom was racking his brain, trying to think what Mr Rafferty would want to see him about. Did everything go alright? What went wrong? Did he want his money back?

There was a knock at the door at precisely half past six. Tom remembered what Foxhall-Trott had taught him: if you are expecting a guest, make sure you are the one to greet them. He took a deep breath and opened the door.

Mr Rafferty stood there with a large smile and his hand outstretched to greet Tom.

Tom shook his hand. "Please come in, Mr Rafferty, how are you?"

"Very well, thank you, Tom."

Tom guided him into the parlour and seated him in the same seat where they'd discussed his presentation.

Mr Rafferty said, "See that plaque you have behind you? Never has a truer word been spoken." He was referring to the Confucius proverb. "Tom, I just had to come and tell you what a success the wedding meal was. Both my family and the in-laws as we sat down at the top table just looked at the place settings and it was like a jigsaw puzzle we had done many times before. We all could not stop smiling at each other as each course was served.

"So, on behalf of the family and my new in-laws, I have come to thank you personally for a gift we now have for life."

"You are very welcome, Mr Rafferty."

Mr Rafferty raised himself up from the chair with the parting words, "I will certainly recommend Mr Toff's Services to anybody that has an important dining event coming up. I am sure people in this area will be talking about how the Rafferty family knew immediately which utensil to use at each course. We could clearly see the other guests trying to follow every gesture we made."

CHAPTER 10
MEETING SAUL AND
DAVINA ROSEN AT JACOB'S CAFÉ

Tom arrived on time for the meeting with the Rosens. He could see Lionel at the rear of the café, beckoning him to come to where he was standing.

"Bruchale, this is Saul and Davina, they have been coming to our café for many years. I will leave you with them."

Both parties, for a brief moment, were left unintentionally studying each other. Tom broke the ice with the greeting "Shalom." Both the Rosens lifted their eyebrows and smiled, replying, "Shalom." Tom had heard this greeting many times when customers walked into Jacob's Café. When he'd enquired as to what it meant, Miriam had told him it meant "peace".

"So, you are the Bruchale that we see so often in the café," said Saul. "Lionel and Miriam have given you a big build-up about the services you offer."

Tom blushed slightly and smiled. "I have been well trained, so I think that impressed the Jacobs."

Saul was of average height and build with wavy dark brown hair, a sallow complexion and round brown eyes. He was wearing a dark jacket and trousers with an open-neck white shirt. In contrast, Davina's hair had masses of black curls with a floral bow on one side. Her eyes were a deep green while her eyelashes were naturally long and black, which enhanced the rouge on her pale cheeks and her red lipstick.

Her floral blouse was tucked into a black pencil skirt with a wide black patent leather belt around the waist. The blouse closely matched the pattern in her hair bow, while her ivory-coloured clip-on earrings and necklace made her look smartly dressed for an evening out at a posh restaurant.

Tom asked them what function they were attending.

"It is going to be our fiftieth wedding anniversary, to be held at the City Hall banqueting rooms," Saul told him.

Fees were discussed and agreed, followed by arrangements to visit the Rosens' home.

TOM'S VISIT TO THE ROSENS' HOME

The first thing that Tom noticed was a small object on the right-hand side of the doorframe with some sort of inscription on it. Tom gave a firm knock using the door knocker.

Davina opened the door. She looked at Bruchale with his sack truck and wicker basket, and memories came flooding back of her late grandfather, who had pushed a handcart around their small village in Germany before the war, selling salt and vinegar.

"Come in, please come in. We are all here."

"Davina, I thought that was your door knocker when I first came to the door," said Tom, pointing to the object on the doorframe.

"Oh, that is on most Jewish main doorframes. It is called a 'mezuzah'. There is a parchment roll inside which has the written text of the *Shema*."

Tom was still none the wiser as to what "Shema" meant, but at least he knew it had something to do with Judaism.

From inside, Saul shouted, "Who is it?"

"Bruchale, of course! Who do you think it is?"

"Bring the boy in, make him welcome."

Saul shook Tom's hand and introduced him to his family, as well as the rabbi and his wife. Tom greeted them all with "Shalom."

Tom asked Saul where he could set up his place setting.

"Bruchale, learn one thing," Saul told him. "As soon as you step over the threshold in this house, Davina is in charge."

Tom had the place setting ready in about ten minutes due to numerous rehearsals.

"If you would all like to come in and stand around the place setting, I will start to explain everything," he said, holding his pointer ready to start. "And I am more than happy to take questions as we proceed."

He started by first removing the small fork on the right-hand side of the setting. "I am removing this fork because it is intended to be used only for a shellfish dish. I'm aware that this dish would not be served at your meal but at least you know why it is there if you attend any other similar functions. If you see this small fork displayed, at least it will give you a signal to raise your hand to the server and request for him not to place that course in front of you."

All those assembled looked at each other with knowing smiles and nods.

Tom went through the whole of his routine, including the accepted correct manners while sitting at a dining table. The party had a few random questions but none that fazed him. The group were talking amongst themselves, with comments such as: "Well, I never knew that—and I would have looked a complete fool if I carried on with what I knew."

When Tom was done, Saul tapped the table with a spoon and announced, "Can we all thank Bruchale for a wonderful demonstration."

There was loud applause.

While Tom was carefully packing away his utensils and crockery, Davina asked if she could help.

"Thank you," he said, "but I have to pack in a certain way to avoid damage while I wheel it home."

"I understand," said Davina.

"You could help in another way," said Tom.

"What's that?"

"Can you tell me a little bit about the Jewish religion?"

"But I thought you were Jewish, Bruchale? Because we have seen you many times in Jacob's Café talking to Lionel and Miriam. They treat you like one of their own."

"I'm very fond of both of them and they gave me the name 'Bruchale', so everybody in the café knows me by that name, but I'm not Jewish."

"Anyway, we all love you at the café, and of course I would be delighted to tell you a little about Judaism," said Davina. "You have already been introduced to the Mezuzah. We basically have three ways of practising Judaism: Orthodox, Reform and Liberal.

"Orthodox Jews are probably the largest group in the UK. They believe that every word in the Torah and Talmud should be followed and not adapted to suit modern life.

"Reform Jews remain traditional but they have adapted their lifestyle to fit in with modern society. This is the group Saul and I belong to.

"Liberal Jews are similar to Reform but believe that observing the mitzvoth—the rules that determine what Jews should do and not do—is more of a personal choice.

"Look, just wait there—I have a pamphlet that the rabbi gives out to our children being taught about Judaism, it is simple but clever. Here, take it.

"We thought the explanation about the shellfish fork was very thoughtful and useful if we ever attended non-Jewish functions," she added. "The rabbi really appreciated that."

Saul popped his head around the door. "Davina, don't hold the boy up; he has to get home—but not before I pay him." He reached into his wallet and took out two crisp one-pound notes. "This is for you, Bruchale. We were all very impressed the way you guided and explained everything to us."

The payment was well above what Tom was expecting. "My fee, Mr Rosen, was one pound for the eight of you."

"Bruchale, I have been in business for over forty years and I have never sold anything that would last my customer a lifetime. What you are selling will last your customer a lifetime, so don't sell yourself short."

"Thank you very much, Mr Rosen. You're very kind."

Tom could not wait to get home to tell his grandad and aunt how much money he had earned for just over an hour's work.

He was trying to eat his evening meal and tell both of them what a brilliant day he'd had.

"Finish your meal, Tom, and we will be all ears," said Grandad.

Tom told them all about the event and what he had learned about Jewish customs and rules.

"Mrs Rosen gave me a small pamphlet about their religion," he explained. "I hope to get a lot of custom from Jacob's Café, so this will help me to understand their traditions and make sure that I don't offend anyone.

"That is important," said Aunt Anja in her usual quiet voice.

CHAPTER 11
TOM'S NEW MODE OF TRANSPORT

Tom could see a strange smile on the face of both his aunt and grandad as they kept looking at each other.

"What's the matter?" said Tom. "Have I said something funny?"

At that, Grandad reached up and took a small roll of brown paper that had a twist at each end from the fireplace mantelpiece.

"This is for you. We both hope you like it."

Sweets had not long come off rationing. Could it be a long stick of rock with a name going right through it? It felt solid, like a stick of rock, very smooth—but an odd shape at one end.

"Well, open it up," said Grandad, just as excited. "Don't keep us all waiting."

As Tom opened up the package, he could see it was shiny and black. "It's a bicycle pump!"

"Exactly," said Grandad. "Let's go out to my shed."

There in the shed stood a black butcher boy's bike with a small front wheel beneath a large wicker basket encased in a tubular metal frame. Tom could not contain himself. He wrapped his arms around both Grandad and his aunt, saying, "Thank you! Oh, thank you both so much. I don't have to push my hand truck anymore."

As Tom looked more closely, he noticed that Grandad had painted *Mr Toff's Etiquette Services* on a metal plate beneath the crossbar.

"Look," said Grandad. "If you undo these couple of screws, it folds over to read 'Abramowizc Etiquette Services'."

"What does the small 'Scrivens the Butcher' sign mean, behind the seat?" asked Tom.

"I promised Mr Scrivens the sign would keep his family name displayed."

"Where did you get the bicycle from? It's perfect for me."

"A few months ago I was walking through the High Street and I saw that Scrivens the Butchers had their windows whitewashed and a sign thanking all customers for their custom over many years. The shop door was ajar and I could see Mr Scrivens tidying up. He explained that none of his family had any interest in carrying on with the business. Towards the back of the shop I could see the butcher boy's bike, so I asked him what he was going to do with it.

"Mr Scrivens said I am not sure yet. I was quick to tell him about your new business venture and the fact that you pushed a sack truck with a wicker basket to customers giving these presentations.

"'Mr Scrivens,' I asked. 'How much would you sell it for? It would make my grandson's job a lot easier.'

"He said, 'Well, it cost me a pretty penny when I bought it but I would like to see it go to a good home. So how would ten pounds sound?'

"I told him, 'Unfortunately that is far too much for me to afford,' and I told him I know it's probably worth that.

"Scrivens said, 'Look, let's see if we can come to some arrangement.' He asked me how much I can afford a week. I told him seven shillings and sixpence at the most.

"'I would be doing the same for my grandson,' said Scrivens, 'so let's call it seven pounds at five shillings a week.' Scrivens held out his hand and said, 'Shake on it.' I did gladly.

"Scrivens then made a strange request. 'Can you put something on the bike to say "Supplied by Scrivens the Butcher"? It will at least feel as though the family business is still going.' I said of course I will.

"I wheeled the bike home on a handshake and a five-shilling deposit. I put it straight into the shed and covered it with an army canvas so that I could work on it while you were out."

Tom flung his arms around his grandad and aunt, saying, "Thank you so much."

All flustered, Grandad said, "Ah, I knew there was something else." He produced a long steel chain and sturdy padlock with a key. "That's to make sure the bicycle stays with Mr Toff's Services."

Tom smiled and gave him another hug.

TOM'S PROMISED COMMISSION TO THE JACOBS

Tom called into the café after he finished his shift with Ginger, carrying his bag of free vegetables. Lionel and Miriam were waiting on their customers as usual. As Tom opened the café door, Miriam caught sight of him.

"Bruchale, come on in. I see you are still working on the vegetable stall. You are very hard working. We are so proud of you, and so are the Rosens. They have been here since you met them."

"That's why I called in, so that I can give you both your commission for introducing me to the Rosens."

"Come sit here," said Miriam.

Tom put a small brown envelope, labelled with 'Lionel and Miriam 4s.0d.', on the table.

"Now, Bruchale, Saul and Davina told us all about your wonderful presentation and who attended, so why the four shillings?"

"They gave me an extra pound, Miriam."

"So we take extra commission because you were so good? No, no, no. Come with me, I will show you something. Lift that small curtain on the counter by the door. The Jewish community call this box a 'pushke'. It is a charity box for our people that have fallen on hard times. Just put the two shillings in there.

"So now you see how it works. We find Jewish customers for you and you put our commission in the pushke box. That's a good circle for all of us. Now sit and I will bring you a coffee and toasted bagel."

"But I haven't reached my third customer yet?"

"We can't hear you," Miriam said, smiling while walking away.

When Miriam brought the coffee and bagel, she said, "I have quite a few more customers for you and I know the rabbi has been mentioning your good work."

Tom told the story about his grandad buying the bicycle from Mr Scrivens, and the sign he'd made that could show 'Abramowizc Etiquette Services' on one side and 'Mr Toff's Etiquette Services' on the other depending on who the customer was.

"You are a clever boy, Bruchale," said Miriam, wagging her finger at him. Lionel gave out a loud laugh, making everybody in the café turn around.

"Sorry," said Lionel. "Bruchale is so funny."

"This is so wonderful," said Miriam. "If only my parents were alive to see the family name displayed around the town. I am looking forward to hearing what my customers say when they tell me there is a new Jewish company in town. I will tell them it is not a new Jewish company, it is me, Miriam Abramowizc—and then I will see their faces."

Lionel just smiled and nodded in agreement.

CHAPTER 12
UPDATING MR FOXHALL-TROTT

During a lunchtime break, Tom knocked on Foxhall-Trott's study door.

"Enter!"

Tom entered his study and asked if he could spare ten minutes to update him on his business venture.

"Mr Larsen, please do," said Foxhall-Trott. "I could do with hearing some cheery news. It is cheery news, isn't it?"

"Oh yes, sir."

Tom updated him in a concise way so as not to take up too much time.

"That is excellent news, Mr Larsen, I have high hopes for you. At the moment I see no signs of this business venture affecting your studies."

"No sir. That's always a priority, sir."

"Good to hear, Mr Larsen, good to hear."

TOM'S FAREWELL TO HELPING GINGER

Tom was building up quite a clientele, from both the enclave where he lived and beyond. There were also the customer referrals from Jacob's Café and the rabbi.

He had to logistically manage his presentations in areas to maximise his fees. The new butcher boy's bicycle made his work quicker and easier; the only small problem was having to change the signage over depending on if he was visiting a Jewish home or not.

Tom was apprehensive about telling Ginger that his business had grown so much that he could not keep his vegetable stall job going, despite how supportive Ginger had been when Tom first told him about the business, many months ago.

Tom was trying to find the right words to tell Ginger, but he knew that Ginger just liked talking straight and to the point.

"Ginger," he said, "my business has really taken off, and I'm finding it difficult to fit in all my work and studies." He told Ginger about Scrivens's bicycle, saying that it made his job much easier, but it was still difficult.

Ginger looked at Tom and gave him a big smile. "You have worked for me for quite a few years. You have been honest, hardworking and reliable. I'm going to miss you. I assume you are telling me you must leave?"

In a very quiet voice, Tom said, "Sorry, Ginger."

"Listen, I want to see your name all over town so that I can tell people, 'That young man started off working for me.' Here, don't forget your bag of vegetables. Don't forget to send the other boy, Joe, before Saturday. I've already told him where to meet you and what to do in his job."

"He will not let you down, Ginger," said Tom.

"If he is half as good as you, I will be pleased," said Ginger. He then pushed two pounds into Tom's hand. "There, that's my contribution to your bicycle."

They both gave each other a hug while holding back a tear.

Tom made his way home, both sad and relieved that one chapter in his life had closed and another was opening.

CHAPTER 13
REFERRALS ARE BOOMING

Tom studied the pamphlet that Davina Rosen had given him about Jewish traditions and items used in a Jewish home. He remembered Foxhall-Trott's lessons, encouraging him to take interest in other customs and beliefs. The area Tom grew up in had already given him a good deal of knowledge about people from the northern Mediterranean and Caribbean area.

His interest in Judaism really impressed his Jewish customers when he commented on their style of menorah or the pattern on the cloth that covered the challah bread and other items he noticed in their houses. He did this in an inquiring way, not a patronising way. The customers were always happy to expand on anything that had caught his interest.

Miriam and Lionel loved the feedback they were receiving about their Bruchale. Tom became well known within the Jewish community and received lots of business from them. He also noticed that Lionel and Miriam had changed the way they had set their tables because their customers had been educated by Bruchale and were reminding them the way Abramowizc Etiquette Services would have laid it out. They would both nod to their customers and say "I know, I know," with a big smile. "Look, we have turned our Bruchale into a monster."

Tom was still also very busy with referrals from his enclave and a little further beyond. He raised his fee to five shillings per guest with a minimum charge of two pounds, and still demand was high for his services.

His new butcher boy's bicycle had made a big difference to his business. Tom's savings account for the family was steadily growing, and he frequently asked his grandfather and aunt what they needed as a treat each month. Not every month, but occasionally they requested a small item. For his grandfather, it could be a small tool for the garden, or for his aunt an accessory for her foot-pedal-driven Singer sewing machine.

These small gifts Tom made to his guardians gave him great pleasure in seeing what a small gesture can do. When they would thank him, he would always say that he could never repay the love and care they had both given him.

CHAPTER 14
SCHOOL SUMMER HOLIDAYS
HAVE ALMOST ARRIVED

Mr Foxhall-Trott told his pupils that when he had attended his public school, there were always some projects or other interests that had to be taken up by the pupils and demonstrated after returning from the summer break.

He addressed the class in a quiet voice. "Gentlemen, what else would you be doing during these long eight weeks of boredom?" There were groans from around the classroom. "I would like to see a summary of each of your projects in two weeks."

A voice piped up from the back of the class. "Where are you going for the summer, sir?"

"My parents invested in a small gîte in the South of France just after the war. My family and I visit there when we can."

Tom said, "What is a gîte, sir?"

"Glad you want to expand your knowledge, Mr Larsen. It is the French word for a small cottage. Nothing very grand, but simple accommodation. The one we own is set not far from a village and the sea."

Most of the pupils had not ventured further than thirty miles from where they lived, including Tom.

"Can you tell us a little bit more about the South of France, sir?" said Ronald "Buster" Jones, wishing to waste a bit of English language lesson time rather than showing a genuine interest.

"Mr Jones, I appreciate that this is a stalling ploy but nevertheless many of your classmates have parents or grandparents that come from around these Mediterranean shores and islands.

"The winters are quite mild and snow is very rare. The days can start to get warmer from late February and get very hot during the summer months, with pleasant warm days even in November. Sea temperatures can be acceptable to swim in during April. There are lots of palm trees offering shade along the promenades and most of the plants are drought resistant. People in general and families will walk along the promenades, particularly during the evenings when the temperatures are a bit cooler."

"What is a promenade, sir?" piped Buster, to prolong Fox-hall-Trott's chat.

"It is a wide pathway, Mr Jones, usually alongside a road but can follow a beachfront, that is used by people, as I mentioned, for a daytime or evening stroll."

He continued, "During the hottest part of the day, usually between twelve noon and three o'clock, most shops will close, although cafés will normally remain open, serving food and cool drinks under shaded umbrellas or canopies. There, Mr Jones, I hope I have given you a small insight into life around the Mediterranean."

"Thank you, sir."

"I believe that diversion has taken me exactly six minutes, which means my English lesson will run six minutes into your lunchtime, gentlemen."

"Oh, sir..." Groans came from every corner of the classroom, although Tom and a few others had enjoyed being transported to what seemed an exotic place for six minutes.

A few more weeks went by, and the summer break was now very close.

The Education Department permitted pupils that turned fifteen before the end of the summer break, or indeed the Christmas break, to leave school and seek employment. A few of Tom's classmates would attain that age during the summer break and were eager to go into the adult workplace.

Foxhall-Trott requested project headings, for those who would be returning, so that he could enter them into a register alongside the pupil's name. Tom had chosen the title "Can an entrepreneur have benefits for a community?".

On the last day of term before the summer break, Foxhall-Trott gave them some advice on where to look for sources of infor-mation for their project. He then gave rather a sombre talk to those pupils that were due to leave school during this summer's break, encouraging them to evaluate their worth and seek out the careers that they want, and to take every opportunity, even if some may fail.

"Do not sell yourself short; regroup and start again. You do not have to follow in the footsteps of other family members, unless that is the career you would prefer."

Tom hung on to this advice, because he would be making that choice during the Christmas break.

The school bell rang out. Foxhall-Trott stood by the classroom door and shook each pupil's hand as they left, wishing them a pleasant summer break. There was a special short chat for each of those pupils that were leaving.

CHAPTER 15
THE SUMMER SCHOOL
HOLIDAYS HAVE BEGUN

The enclave where Tom lived offered no organised activities for children, and there was little or no money spare to spend on any treats. When the Italian ice cream man with his cart and horse rang his bell, this could be heard a few streets away. Children would pester their mothers for enough money to buy an ice cream cone or a cheaper cup of fruit-flavoured iced slush, which was made by using a stainless-steel carpenter's-style box plane to shave the flavoured ice block and pour it into your own cup. Other children would be knocking on neighbours' doors asking if they had any bottles that had a money return on them to share with the owner. Children had to earn their own money. Pocket money, in this locality, was unheard of.

There were also the public parks to explore, where groups of children would play hide-and-seek in the trees and dense vegetation. On the walk home, they'd talk about what they will have for their evening meal, having been out playing all day, quenching their thirst at a stream if they were lucky. Their imaginary sandwiches as they walked would have a filling of corned beef, spam, luncheon meat or brawn, followed by a strawberry jelly. They would walk past tea rooms serving afternoon tea for the toffs and press their noses against the glass fronts, only to be chased away by the waitresses.

The next fad was making a bicycle from spare parts, acquired by knocking on neighbours' doors. A frame here, a wheel and saddle there, and so on. Bogeys were made from the chassis of broken babies' prams that were dismantled and a pair of wheels were attached, situated at each end of a small plank. The wheel axle was secured to the underside of the plank by sturdy nails, allowing the front axle to have centralised arched nails to allow some movement for guiding the bogey with your feet or a rope attached. More elaborate bogeys had a seated wooden orange box and a cushion to sit on.

Some of the other usual fads returned, such as a sudden morning decision to go fishing that day. Money was desperately raised between the group for a bamboo pole, a couple of eyelets tied to the pole, a nylon line, fishing float and fish hook. The group would set off and sit by anglers, who would sometimes tell the group to take their piece of bread off the hook and try one of their maggots. Those anglers would reach into their old army bags and retrieve a used round tobacco tin with a perforated lid. Inside would be a wriggling mass of white maggots.

"There," they'd say. "Put one of them on your hook."

A task not for the faint hearted of the group.

They usually only succeed in sadly drowning the maggot, or at best a fish would take it while they'd lost their concentration talking, but it filled another day out. Sometimes, they'd get to share some of the anglers' sandwiches.

Then it could be a game of marbles, beginning with the house search, trying to find out where they'd stored them from the last summer holidays. There was an unwritten law that large marbles were worth double of the smaller ones, and multicolour ones were a prized possession, to be exchanged for four or more of the single-colour ones.

The girls occupied themselves with skipping ropes or a large piece of rope also used as a skipping rope so that several girls could join in. They'd recite a sequence of repeated chants while entering the revolving rope at the precise moment.

They also involved themselves in recycling crafts, by unravelling unwanted woollen garments and knitting them into other garments. Another method of recycling woollen garments was to obtain a used wooden cotton reel and place four small nails in a square formation around the bobbin hole of the reel. Then, by weaving the recycled stringed wool in a pattern around the four nails, this produced a knitted woollen rope that passed down through the bobbing hole. This weaving continued until the rope was considered to be the right length to sew together to make something useful, like a tea cosy.

One of the other activities that usually occurred during the summer months, to the annoyance of every mother, was the spreading of limestone chippings to resurface the roads. No announcement was ever made by the local council as to when this activity would take place. Suddenly, one morning, a group of council workers would appear in the street with shovels at the ready. A small tanker lorry containing liquid tar with a spreader pipe at the back would be in position to spread tar over one half of the road. This would be followed by the workmen spreading limestone chippings in a sweeping fashion like scattering seeds, followed by a further dressing of limestone dust.

This activity always caused angry housewives to shout profanities at the men for not taking more care, as the chippings and dust would end up on the scrubbed half-moon pavement stones outside their front doors and on their windowsills, and tar would be brought into homes on children's shoes. The men just continued in a robotic movement, completely ignoring these comments, which they had received on every street they entered.

A steamroller would follow to press the chippings into the tar. These road surfaces were never regraded; chippings were just added over the years, resulting in a pronounced camber in the roads. Tarmac tampers were used around lamppost areas, otherwise the angle of the steamroller would knock them over. Delivery vans and horse-and-carts would stay on the crown of the road to avoid their loads shifting on a steep camber.

Tom was well past all the holiday fads, and from a young age, he would always try and find some kind of work that paid money during the holidays by calling in on shops or tradesmen, asking if they needed any help. This was how he'd first got his job working for Ginger on his market vegetable stall. He'd started that job at the age of ten, earning ten shillings per week.

He felt more like a businessman now, running Toff's and Abramowizc Etiquette Services.

Now that the warmer months were here, businesses were serving afternoon teas both inside and in any outside space they had. Tom's business was really taking off, with his well-respected presentations in high demand. Clients who had engaged Tom services for a presentation on the dos and don'ts while attending an afternoon tea said they then felt in full control of the situation regarding what order to eat your food and the pouring of the tea. They said it enhanced their experience. Their glowing feedback was welcomed.

Tom's Post Office Savings account was swelling, even after chipping into the family budget and buying regular treats for his grandfather and aunt.

The summer holidays were now entering their final weeks. Tom had managed to keep on top of his project for Foxhall-Trott.

The project word count had to be no more and no less than a thousand words. Foxhall-Trott said that this stipulation was to ensure that the pupils concentrated on the subject matter by continually deleting words that were unnecessary and adding in words to strengthen the content of the project.

CHAPTER 16
DEVASTATING NEWS
FROM TOM'S GRANDFATHER

The family were going about their daily routine, Tom following up his appointments and presentations, his aunt Anja carrying out housework chores and preparing the evening meal. Grandad was giving the stone walls in the garden their annual coat of white limewash. This achieved a small illumination effect in the rear garden area during the dark winter months.

He would undertake this task by purchasing lumps of lime from the local builders' merchants and letting the lime lumps soak in a tin bath of water for about two or three days, until the lime had broken down into a creamy consistency. He would then apply the creamy solution to the walls with a paddle brush, taking great care not to flick the lime onto his clothes. A small jug of clean water was kept close to hand just in case any lime accidently went into his eyes.

Grandad would often take a stroll up to the town centre hoping to meet some of his old pals that he went to sea with, or he would just enter a regular café and have a cup of tea and a bun.

While walking home on this particular day, he noticed the *Evening News* placard stating:
LOCAL TEACHER TRAGICALLY KILLED IN THE SOUTH OF FRANCE
This stopped Grandad in his tracks. He entered the newsagent's to buy a copy of that newspaper to read at home, but the magnitude of the headline forced him to return to the café to sit down and read the article.

A tragic road traffic accident occurred at around 10 o'clock local time in the small village of le Soleilville approximately twenty miles from St Tropez on the French Riviera.

The person named in the accident was a British citizen named Montague Foxhall-Trott, who was holidaying at the time.

An eyewitness said that: "Le professeur was coming out of the café where he usually had his morning coffee and pain au chocolat. He was ready to cross the road into the orchard where he teaches conversational English free to the villagers. I saw his head turn the opposite way to the oncoming traffic. He stepped into the road and was hit by a large truck. I think he thought he was back in Britain for that split second. Sad, very sad. He was such a wonderful person.

"The villagers thought that his mannerisms and traditions were bizarre, particularly when he was dining, but we would always just shrug our shoulders and say 'Britanique'. Everybody understood this.

"I spoke to a member of his family who told me that, because of Monty's love for this part of France, its culture, and his love of the people in this village, he should be buried in the local churchyard so that the villagers can pay their respects when they want to."

Oscar Higgins, St Tropez. 14 August 1955.

Grandad put the paper down and thought about how to tell Tom this dreadful news about his beloved mentor.

He broke the news to Anja first, who could not offer any advice on the best approach to take in breaking this news to Tom. They both waited anxiously waiting for Tom to return from his presentations.

The front door opened and they could hear Tom bringing his bicycle through the passageway.

The doorknob turned, and in walked Tom with tears streaming down his cheeks. "It's true, isn't it?" he said. "Foxhall-Trott has been killed. I could see the newspaper placards as I was riding home."

Grandad and Anja just nodded in agreement and stood up to put their arms around Tom, saying, "We are so sorry."

Anja laid the table for the evening meal, but Tom said, "I am not hungry at the moment," and went up to his room.

The following morning, they both waited anxiously for Tom to emerge. To their amazement, when he did, Tom had a positive look on his face and sat down to eat breakfast with them.

"We are so sorry, Tom, about the sad news," said Grandad.

"I know, I know you are. While I was up in my room, I could not help thinking about Foxhall-Trott. All the wonderful lessons and life skills he had taught us. The problem was I was not thinking about the terrible loss his family must be suffering.

"One thing I do remember is that I promised him whatever skills he had taught me, I would, where possible, pass them on to the disadvantaged and underprivileged. He said that was a legacy his father taught him. I will also make a promise that one day I will visit his grave in the South of France.

"So, Grandad and Aunt Anja, that is what I will do. I will make sure that I educate myself into a position where I can keep his legacy alive."

Grandad and Anja were so pleased that something good was coming out of something so tragic.

Tom's enthusiasm for life and business had sprung back into life. His visits to Jacob's Café were still delivering lots of referrals. Miriam and Lionel's faces would light up whenever their Bruchale entered the café. Both would always give him a big hug, but Miriam would continue to squeeze him while planting a big kiss on his cheek, only to leave a red lipstick imprint, which she would wipe away with her patterned handkerchief.

Miriam sometimes embarrassed her adopted son by announcing to her customers how much money Bruchale has raised in the last quarter in the 'Pushke' box. They would all clap as Bruchale's face turned bright red.

The last week or so of the school holidays were very busy for Tom before returning to school.

CHAPTER 17
TOM'S LAST TERM IN SCHOOL, 1955

The first morning of the school term had arrived. Tom had laid out his school uniform and leather satchel the night before. Inside was his completed project requested by Foxhall-Trott, which he would now never read. This was a sad moment for Tom.

The school gates and driveway opened to a large playground area. The new entrant boys stood there in an imaginary pen area, in spanking new uniforms and carrying stiff, unused leather satchels. They were constantly looking around them, confused why some of the pupils looked like men in school uniforms.

The teacher on playground duty blew loudly on his whistle and the established pupils took up their positions in lines. The new entrants kept moving around their circle as though they were being contained by a well-trained sheepdog.

"Stand still, you lot!" shouted the teacher. They all froze on the spot. Walking up to them, he shouted, "When this lot have gone in, follow them into the hall and form neat rows in the front."

In the hall, the headmaster, Edwin Lombard-Stoat, cleared his throat and said, "I'm sure many of you are aware that we lost one of our teachers over the summer holidays, Mr Foxhall-Trott. I will be assigning a new form master to his class sometime today."

That was it, regarding any acknowledgement of Mr Foxhall-Trott. It was clear to Tom and others that Lombard-Stoat was still carrying a grudge about the Charlie Croaker incident.

Lombard-Stoat gave his usual speech about the pride of the school and its achievements, finishing with a word to the new entrants about the wonderful academic journey they were about to go on.

There were now only seventeen in Tom's class, after the ones who had reached fifteen years of age had left.

Their classroom door opened and in walked Arlo Spragg with his former university gown sweeping behind him. He was still sporting his RAF pilot's tie and his handlebar moustache.

"Good morning, gentlemen."

"Good morning, sir," was the reply.

"Right, let us do the proper thing, which in my opinion should have been done in the hall when we were assembled. Stand up, gentlemen, and let us stand in silence for one minute to remember our dear friend and wonderful scholar, Mr Foxhall-Trott." When the minute was up, he continued, "Please close any books you may have opened, because I want to spend the entire morning talking about what we have all learnt from Foxhall-Trott, myself included.

"In the staffroom he was known as Monty. I cannot recall a subject he did not know something about, a wonderful brain and a caring human being. I was lucky enough during the war to be alongside these types of chaps when we flew Spitfires and Hurricanes. They came up from Oxford and Cambridge, just young men in their early twenties, full of life and fun but a bit eccentric. I clearly remember one of them taking a Mr Punch glove puppet and a swazzle mouthpiece into the cockpit. If he was lucky enough to score on a Hun, he would put the glove puppet on and speak over the radio with the swazzle in his mouth and say, 'That's the way to do it.'

"Another chap I remember would wear a set of Mickey Mouse pyjamas under his flying suit, and in the top pocket he had a Mickey Mouse fully paid-up membership card, but instead of his photograph being on the membership card he had Hitler's. We often talked about if he was ever shot down over the sea what his rescuers would have though while removing his flying outfit.

"When we went up on a sortie, I was always glad to have one of those chaps watching my back. Wonderful fellows, and Monty was of that breed.

Arlo's war stories brought a bit of light relief to this sad occasion.

"Are you our new form master, sir?" piped a voice from the back of the class.

"I'm afraid not, old boy. I'm here, just like the boy who stuck his finger in the dyke, until the headmaster selects your new master, who will appear after lunch. Anyway, going around the class in a clockwise direction, starting with you Bennett, what are the important things you learnt from Mr Foxhall-Trott?"

Each pupil in turn gave an uplifting story of how he had changed their life in a positive way and how the life skills that he'd taught were a gift for life.

CHAPTER 18
THE NEW FORM MASTER
TAKES OVER FOR THE LAST TERM

The pupils all sat at their desks, awaiting who would appear. Over the lunchtime break there had been numerous suggestions discussed by the pupils regarding which teacher they could have.

Footsteps could be heard making their way along the corridor towards the classroom door. The door handle turned and in walked Charlie Croaker, looking as dishevelled as ever with some folders under his arm. He'd exchanged his grubby tracksuit and stained plimsolls for a grey double-breasted suit and slip-on black shoes. The suit jacket could not be buttoned up because of his large paunch, so the jacket edges formed large points facing downwards just above his knees. The trousers had numerous creases behind the knee. His large belly caused him further problems regarding his shirt. To obtain a shirt size that fit around his midsection, he'd had to obtain one with a large collar size that started approximately three inches down from his chin. His school tie appeared to have been just unrolled.

He threw his folder down on the desk with a large crash, intending to startle the pupils. They did not stir one bit.

"Bennett, open all these windows, let's see if I can get any oxygen into your dead brains."

Bennett did not stir, just gave him a defiant look.

Croaker arose from his chair and flung open all the windows, almost breaking the panes of glass within their frames. "Right, you lucky people, you have me as your new form master and things are going to be very different from now on. None of this la-di-da nonsense."

Skinny Bennett was the first to leave his desk. With his possessions in hand, he walked up to Croaker's desk, looked at him in a pitiful way and walked out of the classroom.

"Where does he think he is going?" shouted Croaker.

With that, all the other pupils stood up, collected their possessions, and left the classroom. Croaker was left sitting there with his mouth wide open.

Skinny Bennett was waiting in the playground where all his classmates assembled.

"Right," said Skinny. "We have all made a joint decision not to accept Croaker as our form master. Agreed?"

"Agreed," shouted the others.

Skinny was the most unlikely rebel you could have imagined. Although he was the current under-fifteen county boxing champion, he was normally quite reserved and timid. It was so obvious that Croaker's disrespectful tone about Foxhall-Trott had got his gander up.

Skinny summoned them to gather around. "Right, gentlemen, we have outstanding annual school reports for the past four years plus, which have been countersigned by Deputy Head Arlo Spragg and the head, Lombard-Stoat. Therefore, gentlemen, the education system cannot dispute that.

"Can we all please meet up at the bandstand in Rosemount Park tomorrow morning at ten o'clock. Please bring fourteen strips of paper with your name and address on them so we all have a point of contact. Now, let us walk out of the school with dignity, in pairs and in step."

Skinny led the group. As they walked past the headmaster's window, Lombard-Stoat, with Croaker by his side, lifted the office sash window and shouted, "You are all expelled! All of you, do not come back."

When Tom arrived home, he explained to his grandad and aunt what had happen in the classroom. Their reaction was, "Well, let us see what happens next."

The schoolboys assembled as agreed at the bandstand in Rosemount Park the following morning, holding the strips of paper with their contact details. Skinny Bennett asked them to make sure everybody had a copy of everyone's details.

He then made an unusual announcement.

"I know that Tom had done an excellent job representing us in Lombard-Stoat's office over the Croaker saga, but I would like to put myself forward as your spokesman when matters develop with this issue. Can I have a show of hands, please, if you support that?"

Every single hand was raised. An extended applause followed.

"The reason I want to do this is because over the past four years, I feel that I have grown from a very shy, insecure boy into a very confident person. This, gentlemen, is down to your support, and especially our wonderful form master Foxhall-Trott. His voluntary lunchtime lectures on public speaking and debating have given us all the confidence to challenge any situation and defend our beliefs."

Another extended round of applause.

"Same time next week, gentlemen, to see if there any updates to discuss."

Just under a week went by, then one morning a brown envelope arrived by post. The printed wording on the reverse side read "The Education Board". On the front side, printed in ink, was "To the Parents or Guardian of Tomas Larsen".

Grandad brought the envelope to the breakfast table and opened it in front of Anja and Tom.

"What does it say, Grandad?" asked Tom.

Grandad read the letter aloud.

Dear Sir/Madam,

We have been informed by the headmaster Mr Edwin Lombard-Stoat that a serious incident took place at Rosemount School on Monday 1st September. We have been informed that your child, Master Tomas Larsen, was involved in this incident.

A hearing by the Board of Education will take place on Monday 14th September at 11 o'clock in Room 201. We require the above-named child to attend. That child may also bring one guardian or parent with them.

Yours faithfully,
Miss Ethel Withers
Chairperson.

"Well, I would like to attend with you, Tom," said Grandad. "If that is ok with Anja?"

"Of course, Dad," replied Anja.

"Thank you, Grandad," said Tom. "You will now be able to see for yourself what a decent bunch of classmates I have. We all look out for and support each other, and that is thanks to how Foxhall-Trott taught us to be decent human beings."

Tom met his classmates at the bandstand. Everybody seemed to be holding a brown envelope.

"Well, gentlemen, our moment has come," said Skinny. "We now owe it to Foxhall-Trott to give a decent account of ourselves in front of the Board of Education."

"Hear, hear, Skinny!" shouted Buster.

"I will prepare our brief, which will concentrate on the fact that our class has been the top-performing class over the past four years. I want you all to bring your annual school report for the past four years. This is just in case any representatives attending from the school may have tweaked some records.

"Finally, can we all please meet at quarter to eleven sharp outside the education offices before entering as a group. I do not have to tell you this, but uniforms are to be spotless, well-pressed and shoes gleaming. This is for Foxhall-Trott."

Everybody in the group was so impressed by the way Alfie Bennett had taken full control of the situation. Before, he would not say boo to a goose and kept very much to a small group of friends of a similar demeanour. Foxhall-Trott's influence and life skills classes had given Alfie so much confidence.

CHAPTER 19
THE BOARD OF EDUCATION HEARING,
MONDAY 14th SEPTEMBER

The morning of the Education Board meeting had arrived. As discussed, the classmates had all assembled outside the offices. While they were waiting, Lombard-Stoat and Croaker just brushed past them with folders under their arms.

At 10.55, Skinny Bennett said, "Right, gentlemen, let us get ready to line up in twos and enter Room 201."

Some of the parents and Tom's grandad followed behind them.

As they opened the door, the boys entered the room quietly in complete silence and in a neat column of twos with Skinny Bennett leading them. Lombard-Stoat and Croaker were watching the faces of the Board's panel. Each Board member looked at each other with total surprise on their face. They were more used to dealing with school dropouts and persistent truants.

Miss Withers, the chair, began by introducing the members of the panel, which consisted of another woman and two men, all with designated roles within the education system.

The parents and guardians were all seated in a designated area at the rear of the room. They were all quietly muttering to each other about the situation. On the other side of the room were other education officials sitting directly behind Edwin Lombard-Stoat and Charles Croaker.

Miss Ethel Withers started the hearing by welcoming everybody.

"Good morning. We are here today to discuss what happen at Rosemount School to result in fifteen pupils from the same class walking out of their lesson in the presence of one of their teachers, Mr Croaker. We will start with the pupils first. How do intend to represent yourselves? Individually or collectively?"

Alfie Bennett stood up and spoke. "I have been elected as the spokesperson, ma'am."

"Very well, and your name?"

"Alfred Bennett, ma'am."

"You may continue, Mr Bennett, starting with the reason why you all elected to walk out of the classroom."

"As you are aware, we sadly lost our form master, the wonderful Mr Foxhall-Trott, this summer. His loss was still very fresh in our minds. Mr Croaker walked into our classroom and, in our opinion, degraded Mr Foxhall-Trott's style of teaching by stating his first remarks, which were: 'Right, you lucky people, you now have me as your new form master, you can forget all this la-di-da nonsense. Bennett, open all the windows and let's get some oxygen into all those dead brains of yours.'

"Regarding his first point, we did not feel we were lucky to have him as a new form master. Regarding his second point, we did not feel that the voluntary lunch hours Foxhall-Trott gave up to expand our knowledge of life skills were 'la-di-da nonsense'. In fact, they have helped us all a great deal in our lives today.

"On his final point, our brains were not dead requiring oxygen. In fact, we have been the top-performing class in the school for the past four years with Mr Foxhall-Trott. This is displayed on the school's honour board within the school's entrance foyer. We have all brought our past annual school reports, showing exemplary marks and comments throughout every subject by other teachers, except Mr Croaker, who taught physical education and sport, and consistently commented each year on every one of us as 'Poor Performance'. Our reports are here, if you wish to see them, signed by both the Headmaster Mr Lombard-Stoat and Deputy Head Mr Spragg.

"Here I wish to comment, if I may, on our school motto, which is imprinted in the headstone above the school entrance. It translates from Latin to: 'Lead by example.' This is something that Mr Foxhall-Trott instilled into us from the first day we met him. I am sure that the representatives from the school and the Board here today would have to agree with that the pupils before you have turned out immaculate in the school's uniform, a standard that was always a legacy of Mr Foxhall-Trott throughout the school day.

"If I may, I will now come back to our school motto. Mr Croaker, over the past four years that we have known him, has always picked out who he thought was the most agile pupil to demonstrate what he wanted to be displayed in gymnastics and sport. We have never witnessed him at any time demonstrating the school motto of 'lead by example'. It is our opinion that all the other form masters performed this motto throughout their lessons, showing us examples of what to do.

"Finally, we also had experience of Mr Croaker filling in for lessons while other masters were ill or away from school for some other reason. He would religiously enter the classroom and, every time, draw a diagram of the human heart on the blackboard, tell us to sketch and annotate it. He would then take a newspaper from his briefcase and turn to the sports pages. He never once taught us any of the core subjects.

"Thank you, ma'am, for listening to me."

"Mr Bennett," said Miss Withers, "I think I speak on behalf of this panel when I commend you on your concise delivery of both you and your colleagues' experiences.

"Mr Lombard-Stoat and Mr Croaker, we now turn to you for your explanation of the events. Mr Croaker, we will start with you first. Is the whole of the statement given by Mr Bennett as to what happened on that morning correct?"

"Err... yes."

"Is the statement about you not demonstrating gymnastic moves to pupils correct, and relying on a pupil to demonstrate the moves for you?"

"Err... yes."

"Is there any reason for that, Mr Croaker?"

"I have gained a lot of weight over the past year and I find some moves a bit difficult now."

"Mr Bennett stated that this situation has existed for the past four years, to their knowledge. Is this true?"

"Err, yes."

"Let us now turn to the matter of when you fill in for other form masters. Is what Mr Bennett described true?"

"To a point. I read the sports page so that I can keep up with what is happening in the world of sport to advise the pupils."

"Your job, surely, is to demonstrate how to carry out these sports activities, not to tell the pupils the latest sports results. Mr Croaker, why have you not taught any core subjects during these lessons?"

"Because I have no qualifications in any of them. I only studied physical education and sports activities."

"Thank you, Mr Croaker, that has been very informative," said Miss Withers. "Mr Lombard-Stoat, we would like to speak to you next. I believe that you received a copy of a letter from Mr Foxhall-Trott that he sent to the Board of Education about the detention incident with Mr Croaker and his pupils' apology letter to Mr Croaker?"

There was a hush around the room. The pupils all looked at each other and gave thumbs-ups out of sight of the panel.

"Err, yes, I did receive a copy, and the contents of his letter were all correct."

"Then there is no need to pursue that point any further. Can you tell the panel when and how you employed Mr Croaker?"

"The previous gym and sports teacher had retired, so I needed to find a replacement quickly. I then approached the Sports Teacher Training College. They told me that Charles Croaker was looking for employment, so I engaged him in 1946."

"Did you request any of his assessment and exam papers from the college?"

"No."

"So, you had no idea of what his strengths and weaknesses were."

"No. I was desperate to fill the position."

"Were you aware that Mr Croaker was not qualified in any of the core subjects when you employed him?"

"No."

"Then do you think it was right to assign him to fill in for other absent teachers?"

"On reflection, no."

"Finally, Mr Lombard-Stoat, when you were counter-signing these annual reports with Mr Spragg for the pupils here today, did you not think it a bit odd that every single pupil in that form was marked down as 'Poor Performance' by Mr Croaker?"

"I should have picked that up, but we were dealing with a lot of reports."

"Thank you, Mr Lombard-Stoat. The panel will now retire for a short adjournment and deliver our findings."

The pupils were all passing their congratulations down the line to Alfie Bennett, who suddenly seemed bashful again.

The panel reappeared and took up their previous positions. Miss Ethel Withers read out the findings of the panel.

"The panel are unanimous in their decision. First, we will discuss the pupils. Mr Bennett, we all agree that in your delivery you left nothing out and added nothing in that was not true. The school representatives agreed with that.

"Our school inspector has verified that the annual school reports are consistently unfair regarding the comments and marks set against physical education and sport. The Board also find that the pupils were entitled to be taught any of the core subjects by a qualified teacher. The Board agrees on this occasion the pupils were entitled to demonstrate that they were not being fairly treated by both their headmaster and physical education teacher.

"To the pupils, we say it is a great sadness that Mr Foxhall-Trott is not here today to witness the fruits of his labour. As pupils you are in our opinion every teacher's dream to turn out into the world. Intelligent, well-mannered and well-spoken. Therefore, the Board have agreed to issue School Leaving Certificates of the highest merit to all of you.

"We know that you only have six weeks left in school but you may, if you so wish, leave school as of today, if you have employment or if you wish to go on some work experience. You may also choose to remain at Rosemount. Please let our school inspector know what your intentions are before you leave this building; he is waiting in room 202 next door.

"That concludes our findings for the pupils. We now turn our attention to Mr Lombard-Stoat.

"We reject your answer that you were desperate to fill the post of a physical education and sports teacher. You knew that the existing teacher was due to retire; therefore, you had plenty of time and opportunity to interview many suitable candidates and check references. The attitude you took, in our opinion, was sloppy and undeserving of your pupils. We are sure you now recognise the problems and unfair treatment meted out to your dedicated pupils as a consequence of this decision."

Lombard-Stoat's head was getting lower and lower the more Miss Withers spoke.

"Therefore, the Board has agreed that you should stand down from your post as of today and we will arrange a substitute headmaster in your place until a permanent headmaster is in post.

"We now turn to Mr Croaker. It is our opinion that you are not fit to be teaching pupils in your current post. Therefore, you will return to the teacher training college to complete a course on physical education and sport over a six-week period to attain the standards we expect from our teaching staff. If you cannot attain those standards within that period, then you will have to find alternative employment out in the marketplace.

"Those are the findings of this hearing. Thank you."

Alfie told his classmates to rise and form pairs. They all left as they had entered: quietly, with dignity and in pairs. They were followed by their parents and guardians.

Lombard-Stoat and Croaker were in a state of shock and remained seated.

When the pupils gathered outside the building, Alfie requested that they regroup tomorrow at ten o'clock by the Rosemount bandstand.

The following morning, the pupils were so pleased with the result that the Board of Education had ruled in their favour.

Alfie spoke first. "We must not gloat; that would not be Foxhall-Trott's style."

A few voices spoke out. "Alfie, you were sensational in that hearing!"

"Hear, hear!" piped Buster, once again.

"Out of interest," said Alfie, "how many are leaving school, as of yesterday?"

Twelve hands went up, including Tom's.

"Well, gentlemen, maybe this is the time to say our goodbyes. Although remember, we all have each other's contact details, and it would be a great shame if we did not all keep in touch."

There were genuine hugs all around as they departed.

CHAPTER 20
A NEW CHAPTER BEGINS
IN TOM'S LIFE

Tom chatted over breakfast about what he thought he would do now that he officially had left school. His etiquette business was thriving thanks to word of mouth in both the Jewish and non-Jewish communities. He now would have extra time to devote to it, but that was not what his future ambitions were.

"Grandad and Aunt Anja, I intend to keep my business going but I also want to educate myself. So, I am going to organise my week so that I can visit the library and night school, where I can take recognised qualifications."

"Whatever you want to do, Tom, we are here to support you in every way possible," said Grandad.

"I know you are, and that is why I love you both so much," said Tom. "I have a School Leaving Certificate issued by the Board of Education that has awarded me the highest possible marks in all the core subjects, and my character paragraph is outstanding. That is all thanks to Foxhall-Trott. The Board were quite aware of what an outstanding teacher he was and the prejudices those two teachers had against us."

"All behind you now, Tom," said Grandad. "Onward and upwards."

Tom enrolled in night school in advanced core subjects. His thinking was to eventually enter a teacher training college. The same day, he registered at the local library. This is where he met the head librarian, Miss Tiggy Knott for the first time.

She was of average height with short dark brown hair and dark brown eyes. Her dress code was very sombre. She wore a cream-coloured silk blouse under a brown button-down cardigan that had her job title and name on a badge pinned to it. The skirt she was wearing was in a tartan-patterned cream colour above her brown kitten-heeled shoes. Her smile was very wide, displaying a set of beautifully formed white teeth. Tom put her age at about fifty years old, but he knew his age judgement at almost fifteen years old could be completely wrong.

There was something warm about her approach to her library members. Nothing appeared to be too much trouble, and she seemed a fountain of knowledge on a lot of subjects. Her staff knew she enjoyed welcoming new members.

She gave Tom the warmest greeting, saying that it was always so nice having a new subscriber to the library. She asked Tom what his interests were and proceeded to show him the various sections of the library he was most likely to use, including the toilet facilities.

Tom noticed a light oak six-panelled door with a gold-lettered "Room 1" on the top section. Beneath that was an information slider, which currently read 'IN USE'. A shiny round brass door-knob provided access. He enquired what that room was used for.

Tiggy replied, "Oh, that is for people doing research. It must be booked well in advance."

She just pointed to the "silence" and "no eating or drinking" signs strategically placed around areas of the library.

"Right, let us go back to where we started, because we have some forms to fill out to get you officially enrolled. I will also explain how many books you are allowed to take from the library and what the penalties are if you do not return them at the correct time."

Various forms were filled out and signed by Tom, and he was given his own identification card with a unique six-digit number.

"There," Tiggy said. "You are now enrolled."

"Do I call you Miss Knott?" asked Tom.

"No, no, everybody calls me Tiggy. And what do I call you?"

"Tom is just fine."

Tom knew that he had to set out a strict routine for himself to manage his studies and business venture. The library opened its doors at nine o'clock until 6.30 in the evening Monday to Friday and closed at 4 o'clock in the afternoon on Saturday.

Tom arrived promptly at nine each morning as Tiggy was unlocking the door. She would say "Good morning, Tom," even before the door was fully opened.

Tom made an agreement with himself that he would not take any library books home, as there needed to be a cut-off point between his study time and his business time.

As the weeks went by in the library, Tom became more curious about Room One. Every morning, the slider on the door was always in the "In Use" position.

At approximately 10.30 each morning, Tiggy would go to the room with a tray holding three mugs and a plate with a teacloth draped over it. Tom would hear a little bit of chatter and laughter just before she came out of the room.

He became more and more fascinated by who was in that room, but he always pushed those thoughts to one side and carried on with his studies.

Almost two months had passed since Tom started visiting the library, so technically he would have now officially left school. His thoughts went back to the Board of Education hearing and the wrongs that were put right at that meeting. He also realised that it would have been at this time he would have been saying his goodbyes to the wonderful Mr Foxhall-Trott, had he been alive.

During this moment of reflection, a great sadness came over Tom as he realised that there would be no Mr Foxhall-Trott to relate his progress and career choice to. For a moment, a voice came into his head: "Well done, Mr Larsen, you are turning into the respectable gentleman I expected you to."

Tom smiled to himself and thought, *I will be a success for you, Montague Foxhall-Trott, Grandad, Aunt Anja and the wonderful Jacobs who gave me my first business opportunity.*

Tom had enquired with the college about subjects that were acceptable (provided he achieved a high enough grade) to gain entry to a teacher training college. They told him that there was high demand from colleges and high schools for teachers with the following qualifications: advanced maths, English language and literature, and economics.

Tom read book after book on these subjects, cross-referencing each detail in his notes with the ISBN number of the book, author and page number. He soon built up an excellent reference system for studying. One of Tom's biggest problems was knowing whether he was studying the correct material required for an eventual entrance to the college exams.

Tiggy did her rounds each day with members of her staff, ensuring that books left on the reading tables by lazy library members were returned to the correct section and the correct shelf. While walking around the library, she could not help herself from looking at what people's interests were. She would pull a small yellow duster from the pocket of her floral overall jacket and linger a little while longer at various reading tables to see what members' reading tastes were. She called it research.

In a very whispering librarian voice, she asked Tom how his studying was going. Tom explained that he had all the material he needed in the library but, with no guidance on how to concentrate on the style of questions within the college entrance exam, he felt he might be devoting too much effort in some areas and not enough in others.

Tiggy just nodded in agreement and placed her hand on Tom's shoulder as a sign of support as she walked away.

Tom kept his business life and studying life separate to ensure he was giving the best to each one. His business life became a welcome distraction from the solitary times spent studying alone, apart from the glancing smiles of the library staff and Tiggy as they went about their daily duties.

Tom always had a moment's pause every time Tiggy went into Room One with the three mugs and the covered plate between ten and eleven o'clock each morning. He thought to himself that he was always the first to enter the library each morning when Tiggy opened the library. He'd never actually seen anybody enter that room, although he had to assume that he spent time searching the subject files and visiting the book sections, so maybe that was when the room was entered.

The months drifted into almost two years and Tom's knowledge on the subjects he was reading continued expanding but he still had no way of testing it.

One day, while Tom was referencing his information at the reading tables, Tiggy stood quietly beside him and placed an opened brown package by him.

She bent over him and quietly said, "Open it. Have a look inside."

Tom could immediately see a large stamp on the package, alongside the Royal Mail postage stamp, stating "The Teacher Training College". The package was addressed to Miss Tiggy Knott at the library's address.

Tom's hands shook as he retrieved the documents inside. All of them had a large blue stamp in the right-hand corner, which read: *DO NOT REMOVE FROM THE LIBRARY. FOR REFERENCE PURPOSES ONLY.*

There was a selection of Teacher Training College final exam papers for the past three years, covering maths, English language and literature, economics, history and science. There was also a set of the past three years' entrance exam papers.

Speaking in a very quiet tone, Tom asked, "Tiggy, how did you get hold of these?"

"I will tell you how I got hold of them later, but when you see me walking around the library with my duster and collecting books—that is my readership research. Each year we are given a budget to spend on library furniture and books. All maintenance of the building is taken care of by the local authority. So, I always have a wish list, that the staff and I discuss, what to spend the budget on. It was you, Tom, that gave me the idea."

"How was that?" said Tom.

"Well, library members are coming here and reading for leisure, reference or, like you, to study but as you said, how can they gauge their studying? So, it was an easy decision. We discussed at a staff meeting that we need more research material, from eleven-plus papers up to university level. So, we spent some of the budget on those papers."

"You are an angel, Tiggy."

Tiggy lifted both eyebrows and gave a wide smile, wagging her finger at Tom, saying, "Make sure you return those papers to the desk every time you use them. Do not remove them from the library."

Tom felt as though he was surrounded by Christmas presents and did not know which paper to look at first. He could not resist flicking through the opening pages of all of them. The excitement just grew as he looked at the first question of the English language and literature paper. He felt he had no problem answering it, but then a little doubt crept into his mind. Did he really have the answer they were looking for, because the question could be interpreted another way? These questions of "What do you think Jack meant when Jill said..." gave Tom doubts, and he knew that exam time was too precious to be wasted on doubting moments.

Throughout the following months, he worked tirelessly, writing out each question in an A4 notebook and putting down his interpretation of the answer. Each notebook was labelled with the subject matter and marked "Finals" or "Entry".

He was so pleased to have so much information at his fingertips, but the nagging questions always in his mind were: Are my answers correct? Is my thinking logical?

Tiggy had noticed a frustrated look on Tom's face for the past few days and quietly came alongside him to ask what was wrong. "You look worried," she said.

Tom explained that he was so grateful for all the information that she had provided him with, but he had this constant doubt that his interpretation of the questions may not be correct.

"Give me a few days to think about that," said Tiggy.

The few days turned into a week, then she told him, "Tom, I think I may be able to help you with your 'Doubting Thomas

Syndrome'. Can you come to the library at eight o'clock on Monday?"

Tom took in a sharp breath and said, "Of course I can."

ROOM ONE

Tom arrived at eight o'clock and was waiting for the library doors to open. The double entrance doors were of a dark, solid oak sectioned into six panels. Gold lettering at the top read "Public Library". A small panel in the door at eye level about the size of a letterbox had an ornate cast-iron grille. On the inside there was a hinged flap to allow the person on the inside to see who wanted to enter.

Tom was both anxious and excited to see what help Tiggy was able to offer. Tiggy opened one side of the large oak doors and beckoned Tom in.

"Follow me," she said. "I am going to take you into room number one."

Tom was tingling all over. He had watched Tiggy take a tray into that room for the past two years. She never knocked before entering; she just gave a muffled cough and the door would open. You could barely hear any voices when the door was closed behind her.

Tiggy was leading with Tom immediately behind her. As they approached Room One, Tiggy opened the door and slid the information slider on the door to 'IN USE'.

"Wait here, Tom. I have some friends I would like you to meet."

Tom had to adjust his eyes because of the brightness from the large multi-paned window at the far end of the room. He could see that the room was an elliptical shape and the ceiling height was double that of the main library.

There were books from floor to ceiling, held on dark-stained wooden shelves and stored in alphabetical order of subject around the room, starting with astronomy. Each subject was subsectioned from top to bottom into categories.

On each side of the window was positioned a narrow staircase displaying a sign stating 'ONE PERSON ONLY'. These stairs led up to a narrow balcony surrounding the upper part of the room, providing access to books stored at the higher levels. Tom was completely mesmerised.

From the ceiling hung four large cream-coloured globed lights that were supported by chains intertwined with the fitting's electrical cables. Two were placed at a higher level to shed light onto the balcony while the other two hung about four feet above the long reading table and chairs. An open-top cabinet beneath the large windowsill held a bibliographic index system, specific to the subject matter contained in this room.

As Tom closely examined the room he noticed an anteroom to the side, the door of which displayed 'STAFF ONLY' in white lettering.

While Tom was standing there, Tiggy re-entered the room. "Right, my staff are all going about their duties so I want to introduce you now to some friends I met while I was at university."

With that, she gave her usual muffled cough, and opened the door labelled 'Staff Only'. Tom could not see anything at first because the small side window permitted very little light, producing almost a smoke-like haze around the perimeter of the room. He could make out some figures sitting at a wooden table. The figures started to fold their newspapers into sections, leaving the editorial they'd been reading uppermost on the folded section.

"Tom, I attended university with these gentlemen a few years before the war started, and we have been loyal friends ever since," said Tiggy. "This is Archibald Brine. He taught maths and science."

"Hello Tom," said one of the men. "Tiggy has told us a lot about you and your aspirations. They call me Salto."

Salto had grey wavy hair, round sparkly brown eyes, a ruddy complexion and was clean shaven. Height about average.

"This is Augustus Summers. He taught English language and literature."

"Hi Tom. Just call me Gus."

Gus was quite tall with thinning grey hair, pale blue eyes, a sallow complexion and a facial expression that displayed a troubled life.

"Finally, let me introduce Sebastian Drinkwater."

"I'm Seb, economics and history."

Seb was continually smiling while introductions were being made. He was short and rather rotund, with brown curly hair, brown eyes and a brown moustache.

Tiggy turned on her heels and said, "Tea and snacks at the usual time," as she left the room.

"Thank you, Tiggy," they chorused.

Tom quickly studied the three men in front of him. Their clothes were clean but none of their garments matched. Their shoes were neatly polished but with odd-coloured laces against the shoe colour.

"Well, young man," said Salto, "let us see if we can help you to achieve your goal. Tom, you must be wondering what we are all doing in the library. We all reside in a charity hostel for men that provides us with a breakfast each morning, an evening meal and a clean, warm bed, but we have to leave the hostel during the day. Our sartorial dress code is the courtesy of the general public, therefore we are very grateful for all the help we receive, including the wonderful Tiggy, who provides shelter, warm drinks and snacks during the day. We all have different stories of how we ended up in a charity hostel, but we feel that subject is still very raw, so we keep it very private. We have not even told Tiggy; she just accepts us as we are, bless her."

"I feel so honoured to meet you all," said Tom. "I could not have dreamt of meeting a group of academic minds who are prepared to give up their time to teach me these subjects."

"Well, it's a long time since we heard such praise," said Gus. "I think we are going to get along just fine and, more importantly, help you achieve your goal."

"Tell us a little bit about yourself, Tom?" said Seb.

He went on to tell them about his family background and his part-time job with Ginger, but he took great care in explaining the information about his hero: Montague Foxhall-Trott.

He told them that Foxhall-Trott's voluntary lunchtime lessons had inspired him to start up his etiquette business with the help of the Jacobs, Lionel and Miriam. There was a chorus of "well done" from his newly introduced tutors.

Salto suggested that it may be more productive if his tuition was split into two morning periods per week, consisting of a Monday–Wednesday and Thursday–Friday, alternating them each week. This would allow Tom to attend to his business in the afternoons.

"How does that sound, Tom?"

"Perfect," was the reply.

The Passover Club (that is what the vagrants nicknamed themselves) asked Tom to give them as many examples as possible of the main sticking points he'd been encountering in all the subjects and hand them in to Tiggy before next Monday.

Tom noticed that their stay at the hostel, not due to their poor choice of lifestyle but because of unfortunate circumstances that had happened during their life, had not diminished their skills in vocabulary or speech. They still spoke with Received Pronunciation, also known as BBC English. Foxhall-Trott had sounded even posher, like the Pathé News readers in the cinema. Tom thought it would be a good idea to ask them to correct his speech mistakes when they occurred and to help soften his local accent.

It was agreed between the Passover Club in this initial meeting that Salto would take the first Monday–Wednesday morning, Gus the Thursday to Friday, and the following week would start with Seb on Monday and so on, alternating each week. Tom laid out on paper some of the problems he was having with the subjects.

"So next week, gentlemen," said Salto, who for the time being seemed to be acting as chairperson, "we start our programme with Tom. And thank you, Tom, for submitting the issues you were facing with some of the subjects. We will look at these and hopefully find the solutions."

That week seemed a long time for Tom.

On one of his visits to Jacob's Café, he was greeted by the usual hug and kiss on the cheek from both Lionel and Miriam.

"First, sit and tell me, Bruchale, how are you?"

Tom told them all about the help he would be receiving from the Passover Club at the library.

"These vagrants are Jewish?" Miriam asked.

"No, Miriam, they have just called themselves that because they feel they have been passed over in life."

CHAPTER 21
TOM'S TUITION WITH THE VAGRANTS

Monday morning arrived and Salto was waiting in the anteroom with the others, who were both reading the daily newspapers.

"Tom, your maths and science questions that you provided will be relatively simple to resolve, but that is just for passing an exam question. If your ambition is to teach at a grammar school then you need to know when and where these subjects began in the western world. Maths and science have been in existence for thousands of years.

"Open your notebook and write down the following: Babylonian, Egyptian, Greek and Roman. Then I want you to write down Newton, Leibniz, Euler, Gauss and Einstein. If you read about these subjects and the characters I have named, you will find many of the answers to your questions in their research.

"I will deal with one of the questions you submitted, because I want you to think in a different way. Here is a sketch from a past paper of a thirty-foot high flagpole with the flag fluttering in the wind, showing a wind force of fifty pounds against the flagpole. Calculate the section size required of the flagpole so that it does not to fall to the ground."

Tom was concentrating hard on Salto's voice.

"Now, Tom, I want you to turn your sketch ninety degrees to the right and tell me what you see."

"The flagpole is leaning out like a cantilevered flagpole," Tom said with a smile. "So, I use the formula for a cantilevered section of timber."

"Exactly." Salto smiled. "Always try to look at problems from a different approach."

Gus then folded down his newspaper and turned towards Tom. "Right, young man. I believe, like Salto, that research is the key. It will also put you in good stead for university. We will be looking at modern English language from 1603 to 1900. Regarding

Shakespeare's work there are plenty of books on both his life and works; therefore, I have no intention to dwell on his subject.

"I would like you to write an essay of two thousand five hundred words, no more and no less, on any topic you choose, but I want to read plenty of descriptive and conversational sections in it." Tom's thoughts turned to Foxhall-Trott's lessons regarding exact word counts. "I would suggest you read *Jamaica Inn* by Daphne du Maurier. The descriptive writing within will give you some idea of what I am looking for in your essay."

Seb had listened quietly as his two colleagues gave advice, and now it was his turn.

"I agree with the same principle as Salto and Gus. If you are intending to teach at a grammar school, you need to be up on your game because the little blighters will try and find chinks in your armour if they can. However, I think we all agree, if you do not know the answer to a question, be honest and say you don't know but you will find out the answer.

"The reading subjects I would suggest for economics are: a little on the ancient Greeks, Xenophon and Aristotle. The Middle Ages: Thomas Aquinas and Duns Scotus. The sixteenth to eighteenth century: school of Salamanca, Jean Bodin and Thomas Mun. The nineteenth to early twentieth century: Sidney Webb, and Keynesian logic.

"For history: Greek and Roman. Medieval Europe. The Tudor and Georgian periods. Modern history, the 1900–1950s.

"We appreciate it is not going to be easy, Tom, but remember we have all been through this before and at university. We intend to train you beyond the teachers' entrance exam. We are preparing you for a university degree. We all intend to test and problem solve in manageable chunks, because we are aware you also have a business to run while you study."

There was a quiet cough outside the main door to the research room. Salto got up from his seat and opened the door. "Ha, wonderful, Tiggy. Shall I take the tray?"

On the tray were four mugs of tea and some buttered scones.

A large smile came across Tom's face as he realised, he was now part of a special group.

"How are you settling in, Tom?" enquired Tiggy.

"He will be fine," said Salto. "We have all given him plenty to work on. Let us reconvene in say one month. By then, Tom should be able to show me some of the maths problems he has solved."

Tiggy mentioned to Tom, "You have unrestricted access to use the research room as and when you need to, but remember no books are to be removed from that room.

CHAPTER 22
NOSE TO THE GRINDSTONE

Tom knew that the only way to tackle all these subjects was in small chunks. He scheduled time to study each subject during his mornings at the library, devoting two hours to each subject throughout the week, keeping a detailed account of his study notes.

His afternoon business became a welcome relief to the studying. He was able to have a coffee and bagel with Lionel and Miriam, chatting with their regular customers. Aunt Anja was also taking down his future bookings at home with people that would call in person.

It was what Tom enjoyed doing the most, but he realised that an education was not going to be offered to him on a plate. He would often reflect on his time with Foxhall-Trott and think in his mind, *What would you do, sir?*

The same answer would always come back. *Mr Larsen, knowledge is a key that can open many doors.*

Thank you, sir.

The studying, followed by testing carried out by Salto, Gus and Seb, continued. So did the mugs of tea and snacks supplied by Tiggy.

Close bonds soon grew between the four of them. The Passover Club felt that they had regained their enthusiasm for teaching and were constantly looking for new challenges for Tom in the various subjects. When it was not their days for teaching Tom, the other two of the Passover Club were always discussing his progress. Their daily newspapers were now rarely picked up.

TOM HAS UNIVERSITY IN HIS SIGHTS

Two years had passed of tuition with the Passover Club when Gus entered the anteroom with a large smile on his face. Everybody around the table was puzzled.

Gus sat down and turned to Tom. "Did you say your grandfather was Danish?"

"Yes," replied Tom.

"Born in Denmark?"

"Yes, he was, Gus."

"Excellent!" replied Gus, slapping his thighs.

The group were none the wiser as to why all these questions were being asked.

"Well, gentlemen, I bumped into Reggie Wainscote, head of university admissions, on my way here."

Salto and Seb nodded. "Oh, Reggie."

"He asked me what I was doing now, so I told him that the three of us were doing funded research work in the library."

"Well done, Gus," said Salto.

"If he ever needed to get hold of us, I said, see the head librarian Miss Tiggy Knott and she will make sure the information gets to us."

"Good thinking, Gus," Seb and Salto said together.

"I also told him that we have been tutoring a bright young boy named Tomas Larsen for the past two and a half years. Well, listen to what he said.

"He said, 'Larsen? Sounds Scandinavian to me. Is his mother, father or grandparents Scandinavian? If so, he can obtain a dual nationality passport and he can then apply for an entrance exam to the university as a foreign student. If he passes, he will be accepted with student fees paid during his course by the Danish Government."

Tom could not stop smiling. "University. I could be going to university."

"We all still have our qualifications, Tom, so we are entitled to give an authorised signature that in our opinion you have attained a standard to apply for the entrance exam. I have arranged to meet Reggie tomorrow morning for the entrance exam papers to be filled in. An entrance exam date has been set for four weeks' time."

Turning to Tom, Gus said, "Tell your grandad to get you a dual nationality passport as quick as possible. We will all get you into university yet."

Tom said, "I am so excited. Do you mind if I leave now to go and tell Grandad and Anja?"

"Not at all!" they all shouted.

"It means more of Tiggy's snacks for us," added Salto.

When Tom arrived home, he was breathless.

"Grandad, Anja, come quick and sit down."

He told them the whole story from start to finish. They both rushed over and gave him a group hug.

"Well done, Tom," said Grandad. "You have worked so hard. I could not be a prouder grandad.

"Well, let me find my Danish passport, birth certificate and other information I have confirming that I was born in Denmark, and so was your father.

"Let us go to the Danish Consulate first—it is in a group with other consulates in the docks area—and ask them what information they require to obtain your dual nationality passport. It is important that you come, Tom, because you will remember what they ask for."

The two returned a few hours later with the necessary papers and information. Their first appointment was with a studio photographer to have Tom's black and white photographs taken for the passport. The back of each photograph was signed by the local MP as a witness to the true likeness of the person. He also witnessed Tom's signature on the application form.

The consul told them to bring four photos for passport use and two attached to the application form straight back.

They arrived back at the consulate, and it was the first time that Tom had heard his grandad speaking fluently in Danish. The consul was brought up about fifteen miles from where Grandad was born, so they were at home talking about various places in that locality, telling Grandad what had changed.

Everything was in order, so Tom's passport was signed and stamped by the consul.

"There, Tomas Larsen, you are now a true Danish Viking. But now I want you to take some books that will inform you more about Denmark, its people and its language, and I am sure your grandad can help you with that.

"Now you know where I am, I hope you will pop in now and again. By the way, Tomas, we will also be glad to help with your studies. Tell the university to send any accounts requiring payment directly to me. You can also do the same with receipts for any official course books you require."

Tom felt as though Christmas had come early. Grandad turned to Tom and hugged him, saying, with a tear running down his cheek, "I wish your mother and father could have been alive to see this day."

"Grandad, I am so excited. I want to call in and see the Jacobs to tell them my news."

"Ok. I will make my way home and tell Anja all about it. I will see you at home later."

Tom had a kick in his step as he made his way to Jacob's Café.

"Lionel it is Bruchale! Coffee and a bagel please, don't forget the honey." Miriam planted her usual big kiss on Tom's cheek, pinched his cheek and gave him a big hug.

"How is my Bruchale?"

"I have just had the best morning ever, Miriam."

He told her and Lionel all about Gus of the Passover Club's chance meeting with Reggie Wainscote, head of university admissions, and his new Danish passport.

"Oh, this is so wonderful news, my Bruchale. My Bruchale will be going to university!" she shouted across the café.

Heads looked up from what they were eating, and people clapped and nodded in approval.

Tom was embarrassed and just nodded back, saying, "Shalom, shalom."

"Miriam, I am not there yet," he told her. "I have to pass the entrance exam first."

Lionel was trying to calm Miriam down, saying, "Bruchale will take it a step at a time."

Tom was nodding in agreement in the background.

Miriam calmed down a little and started talking about these wonderful men in the Passover Club. "Such talent going to waste. For me they are all mensch."

Tom smiled. "Miriam, what is a mensch?"

"It is a Yiddish word we say for a person who has integrity, who is reliable and supportive."

"Well, they are certainly all of those," said Tom. "Miriam, Lionel, I have been thinking for a long time—how can I ever repay the Passover Club for the kindness and help they have given me? They have so many skills between them, and I do not want them to be wasted."

"I could not agree more, Bruchale. What are you thinking?"

"I am thinking 'Abramowizc and Toff's Tutorial Services'. What do you think?"

"My Bruchale is a genius." Miriam gave him another big kiss on the cheek.

Lionel gave a muted cough and said, "Have you discussed this with the Passover Club?"

"Not yet, but I hope they will embrace the idea of doing something they love, while gaining respect for themselves and helping others."

"My father would always say 'Do yourself a bit of good without doing anybody any harm.'"

Lionel nodded in agreement with Miriam.

"Well, I must go and tell the Passover Club my good news," said Tom.

He walked into the research anteroom just as Tiggy was bringing in the tea and snacks. She only had three mugs on the tray. "I will go and fetch another mug of tea, Tom."

"No, wait a minute. I want to show everyone my new Danish passport."

"Well done, Tom. We are all so pleased," came from the foursome.

"The Danish consul also told me that the Danish Government would fund my course and any authorised course books."

"Right," said Gus. "Let us double check your submission papers for the entrance exam to ensure that they are in order before I hand them to Reggie tomorrow."

Each member of the Passover Club ensured that every question was completed including their signature boxes and Tom's new Danish passport number. Gus called Tiggy and asked her to double check the papers.

Two days later, Reggie Wainscote called in to see Tiggy and confirmed everything was in order, giving her the exam venue and time for Tom to arrive. He also asked Gus to give Mister Larsen his exam identification number to be written on each paper he sits. There was also a pamphlet telling the student the only things that are allowed into the examination hall.

To settle his nerves about the forthcoming exam, Tom turned his mind to the tutorial idea for the Passover Club. He waited for Tiggy to bring the usual morning tea and snack. She gave her muted cough and entered the anteroom. As she placed the tray on the table, Tom said, "I have a business proposition to put to the club. Tiggy, please stay—I think your view would also be important."

As the three club members were taking their mugs and picking a snack, their eyes were all fixed on Tom.

"You have all spent a couple of years coaching and encouraging me to attain a university degree," he said. "So how can I ever repay your gifted kindness?"

They all just shrugged their shoulders and Gus said, "We have really enjoyed it, and it has taken the boredom out of our lives."

"I called in to see the Jacobs, and they said what I have been thinking all the time you have been coaching me: what a waste of talent. Miriam said you are all mensch, every one of you."

"Mensch? What is a mensch?" enquired Salto.

Tom explained and watched a smile return to their faces.

"Absolutely," said Tiggy.

"Well, how do you feel about the Passover Club running their own tutorial school?" Tom suggested.

The three of them turned to each other and Seb said, "But how? Where? What about decent clothes to wear? The hostel?"

"Leave all that to me and the Jacobs. All I am looking for at this stage is that you are interested."

They all put their arms around each other's shoulders and said, "Yes!"

Tiggy was clapping her hands like a seal waiting for its next fish meal.

CHAPTER 23
ENTRANCE EXAM DAY AND THE BIRTH OF TUTORIAL SERVICES

Tom's entrance exam day came and he passed with a distinction, giving him the opportunity to study in his local university. He would not start his three-year degree course until late September, giving him time to start thinking about setting up the tutorial service.

This took many visits to Jacob's Café, discussing this new business venture with Miriam and Lionel. Miriam was the driving force networking with her customers for all the assistance she could get for the Passover Club.

One customer stood out above the others: Samuel "Sammy" Kaye, who had a vacant business premises at the very end of the High Street which had very little footfall. It had been vacant for over eighteen months.

When Sammy came into the café for his regular hot lemon tea and toasted bagel, Miriam put his order down on the table and said, "Sammy, this is on the house."

Sammy looked up and said, "Miriam Jacob, are you trying to schmooze me? What are you after?"

Miriam sat down beside him and told him all about Bruchale and the Passover Club and how they all wanted to run a tutorial service. "There is not one in the city, Sammy, it will be a gold mine."

"Miriam, let me think this over. Did you say Bruchale wants to do this?"

"Yes, it was his idea to try and find a way to help the Passover Club and put their talents to good use."

"I like Bruchale very much. The money he has put into the pushke box, including you and Lionel, to help others is heartwarming. I will see you as usual in the morning and give you my decision on the premises."

Miriam could not rest all day, pestering Lionel with the same question: "What do you think Sammy will say?"

Lionel always gave the same reply: "He is a businessman."

The next day arrived. Sammy came in at his usual time and placed the same order, leaving the correct money on the table. He showed no facial emotion.

Miriam brought his order over and placed it down. As she turned, Sammy said, "Miriam, sit. You, Bruchale and the Passover Club can rent my place."

"Oh, Sammy, this is wonderful news."

"Wait. Listen to the terms and conditions."

Miriam sat closer to him to listen. Lionel was walking almost sideways to his customers while trying to listen to their conversation.

"There are three bedrooms, a toilet and wash-hand basin on the first floor. The ground floor has three good-sized rooms, a kitchen and a separate toilet. It is all furnished but will need a clean.

"Now, the rent. You will pay me..." Miriam's body was beginning to tighten up. "...nothing. For the first six months, but you will paint the inside. After the six months, you will pay me half rent at eight pounds per calendar month for one year, and four per cent of your takings. After that year, I will drop the four per cent on the takings. You must pay all the utility bills, but I will make sure that the electrical, gas and plumbing are all in good working order before you occupy."

"Sammy, you are a true mensch." Miriam leaned over to hug and kiss him on the cheek.

Sammy leaned backwards, saying, "Miriam, I am a married man!" to roars of laughter in the café.

Tom visited the café to find out about the outcome of Miriam's meeting with Sammy.

"Bruchale, wonderful news," she told him. "Sit and I will tell you. Lionel, coffee and a bagel please."

Tom was so excited that there was a possibility of getting the tutorial services up and running before he started his first semester at university.

"Miriam, we must now think about furnishing the ground floor as a teaching area. Second-hand goods will do until we can replace them."

"I will speak to the rabbi to see if any help can come from the congregation."

Within two weeks, they had more furniture for the premises than they needed.

Tom invited the Passover Club and Tiggy to come and see what had been achieved. Salto, Gus and Seb's jaws dropped as they explored the premises and dreamed about how their lives could now change for the better.

This was the first time that Miriam and Lionel had met the Passover Club and Tiggy. Tom's grandfather and Anja also turned up.

Miriam gave her usual big hug on greeting them, saying, "You are the wonderful people who are helping my Bruchale. It is so nice to meet you all—and you," she added, hugging Grandad and Anja.

The group looked at each other and looked at Tom for an explanation.

"I have known Miriam and Lionel for many years," he said, "and they have always called me Bruchale. It means 'little blessing'."

"Everybody in the Jewish community knows my Bruchale," said Miriam proudly.

All the introductions were made, with the Passover Club stating what subjects they would be teaching.

Miriam put her arm around Anja's shoulder and said, "You, my princess, will have the most important job of all: greeting the little darlings and their parents as they arrive. For you, we have this beautiful reception counter and chair. The rabbi has donated a beautiful white phone that will be connected soon."

As a surprise to all the guests, Miriam pulled back a white tablecloth, revealing a whole range of foods from her café. "Enjoy, we are a new family now."

The Passover Club had never felt more wanted in the community. Tiggy had tears flowing down her cheeks with happiness for them.

The rabbi and Sammy popped their heads around the entrance door with greetings of "Shalom, shalom."

Soon the whole group were chatting and laughing, something the Passover Club had not done in a very long time.

As Tom awakened the next morning, Miss Ethel Withers popped into his head. She was the Board of Education chairperson at the School vs Pupils hearing.

Tom called at the offices to enquire if she was still in post there. She was. He asked the receptionist if he could arrange a future meeting with her, explaining the education case she'd chaired.

"Wait there," was the reply. "I will go to her office and find out."

The receptionist came walking back with a slight smile on her face, followed by Miss Ethel Withers.

"Well, well, Mr Tomas Larsen. I remember the case very well. What are you doing with yourself these days?"

Tom briefly explained everything about his business venture that had been operating for a few years and his forthcoming university degree. He went into more detail about the Passover Club and the help from the Jewish community to start a tutorial service, which was the main purpose of his visit. He was aware that post-war class sizes could be as many as thirty-five pupils, and it was not always possible for teachers to devote extra time to those pupils who could not keep up.

"I have brought the tutorial teachers' qualifications and the subjects they specialise in, but obviously they can cover all subjects across the board at a certain level," he explained. "We would be delighted to provide our services to those pupils and bring them up to speed. We would follow your education system regarding enrolment, recording attendance and progress. I have also taken the liberty of providing a fee scale that I trust is acceptable, but I am always willing to discuss."

Miss Withers looked at the Passover Club's qualifications and commented, "I went to the same university." She was nodding and smiling while reading them.

"I remember your case very well," she said eventually, "and I am pleased that my judgement was totally correct. Both you and the other pupils were victimised by people we trusted in our education system. Come and see me at eleven o'clock tomorrow and I will give you my response."

Tom went back to Jacob's Café and explained to Miriam and Lionel what he had been discussing with Ethel Withers.

Miriam pulled out her floral handkerchief and partly covered her mouth, saying, "Oh Bruchale, this would be wonderful business and help the children to a better education."

Tom also visited the library to inform the Passover Club and Tiggy.

Everybody had their fingers crossed for the meeting the following morning.

Tom arrived with as much material as he could think of that could help in his pitch to Ethel Withers. There were two other members of Ethel's team sitting alongside her. Tom recognised their faces. They'd been with her during his Board of Education hearing. Tom was relieved that they all seemed to have smiles on their faces.

Ethel Withers welcomed Tom and went on to talk about how education is so important in the development of young minds. She also touched on the wonderful teaching qualities of Montague Foxhall-Trott and the fact that the panel had a shining example of that educational development before them.

"Mr Larsen, we have decided that we are prepared, subject to visiting your premises, to try a one-month trial. We also agreed that your fee scale is pitched too low, and we have outlined in this document what we consider to be a fair rate for the job. The panel have discussed that there is a slot in our diary in two weeks' time at eleven o'clock. Is that acceptable?"

"Of course. We will be delighted to welcome you and introduce you to the tutorial staff."

Tom left their building and walked briskly, sometimes trotting, all the way to the library first and then to Jacob's Café, telling them the good news.

"We must look our best," said Tom. "We just cannot fall at the first hurdle."

"Benny," said Miriam. "That is who we need."

"Who is Benny?" asked Tom.

"One of the finest Jewish tailors in the city. You have met him many times in the café, Bruchale. You will recognise him straight away. He is always dressed immaculately. He visits for his lunch."

Benny arrived at his usual time, placing the same order.

"Ah, Benny, can I get you anything extra?" enquired Miriam with her arm around Benny's shoulder.

"Miriam Abramowizc, I have known you since our school days, and I know what the arm around the shoulder and that quiet tone in your voice means. Poor Lionel did not see it coming, Miriam."

Lionel smiled and nodded as he walked past.

"Miriam, now get to the point. My food is getting cold."

Miriam started to explain about the new tutorial service and the Passover Club, including the pending visit by the Board of Education.

"Sammy Kaye told me all about it," said Benny, "and that his premises will host these services, including accommodation for the Passover Club. What do want from me?"

"Well," said Miriam, "you are the finest tailor in the city..."

"Stop," said Benny. "What do you want?"

"Clothes for the Passover Club. They are dressed in charity clothes at the moment, with nothing matching."

"Miriam Abramowizc, it is your lucky day."

Miriam smiled. "Lionel, more coffee for Benny—and no bill."

"Miriam, I recently purchased a bale of navy pin-striped cloth at a ridiculous price, just because the white line in part is slightly wavy. It is an excellent, strong weave that will last for years when turned into a garment. Tell your Passover Club to come and see me in the morning. Now, can I finish my food? And no lipstick on my cheek."

Miriam told her Bruchale to ask the Passover Club to be at Benny's Tailoring first thing in the morning. Tom went with them and introduced them to Benny.

"Shalom, Bruchale, come on in. How are you? Busy, I see."

"Benny, I really appreciate what you are doing for us at such short notice."

"Bruchale, I am doing it so that I can eat my lunch in peace at Jacob's Café. And besides, these are good people."

It had been a long time since a stranger had uttered those words to any of the Passover Club.

Benny turned the sign on the front door of the shop to read 'BACK IN HALF HOUR'. He then asked the Passover Club to remove their jackets and put them out of sight in the back room. He then proceeded to take measurements, carefully writing them down in his customer details book.

"I take great pride in my work," remarked Benny, "so not a word to anyone while the fitting is being done and the garments are being made."

The Passover Club made several visits to Benny's over a period of a week. They kept to their word, uttering not a word to anyone.

CHAPTER 24
THE BOARD OF EDUCATION
VISIT TUTORIAL SERVICES

Tiggy had been extra busy bringing academic books that were out of print, but still had a lot of mileage left in them, for tutorial purposes from the library basement to the tutorial services premises. These were placed on bookshelves around each room, carefully indexed and in subject order. She also found some illustrated posters on all kinds of subject matter, from biology to mathematics and the environment. These gave an academic feel to the ground floor rooms.

Finally, the day had arrived for the Board of Education visit. Miriam and Lionel had laid out a small buffet of Jewish fare.

The Board members walked around the premises, paying attention to each area and exploring the educational facilities, ensuring it suited all levels of education. Tiggy had anticipated this and made sure a range of material was on hand.

Tom started by introducing the members of the staff. Anja was introduced as the receptionist. She showed them the system of enrolment, attendance and progress reporting. These systems had been sourced by Tiggy from a top educational department. Smiles and approving nods were received from the guests.

The biggest surprise was the introduction of the Passover Club in their newly designed tutorial outfits created by Benny's Tailoring. Tom had previously discussed with them that their accustomed names used in the library would not suit a tutorial environment. So, Salto became Mr Adams; Gus, Mr Bentley; and Seb, Mr Carlton. Tom and Tiggy found their new names amusing, while trying not to slip up and use their old names.

The Passover Club walked into the room one behind the other, led by Mr Adams.

What a sartorial feast for the eyes. Benny had designed a full-length coat in a navy pinstripe material with a mandarin collar and, to save wearing a shirt and necktie daily, a deep red silk cravat with an A & T logo printed on the front. A small top pocket on the front of the jacket had a flap with "A & T Tutorial Services" embroidered in deep red. The coat tapered in towards the waist, the buttons concealed behind a flap. An inside pocket was tailored into both sides of the jacket with sufficient material so as not to make any concealed writing implements bulge outwards. Hacking jacket-style pocket flaps were placed on each side for decorative rather than functional purposes. Benny obviously wanted to maintain clean lines on the coat. The sleeves had stitched-in white cotton shirt cuffs, with a narrow-band edge in red, to match the top pocket logo. Behind the sleeve were two rows of four small buttons, which represented everybody involved: the Passover Club, Bruchale, Tiggy, Miriam, Lionel and Benny.

Generous pleats were placed into the back panels above and below the fitted waistband to allow for plenty of movement in a seated or bending position. Benny had also made the trousers of the same material, ensuring the leg width was narrow to give a smarter appearance. There were no turn-ups to the bottom, but he introduced a small slit to each side, allowing the trouser to drape over the front shoelaces and the back of the heel to the well-polished black shoes.

They all looked so professional and their outfits gave them a newfound confidence.

The Board mingled amongst the hosts while visiting the buffet table. Their friendly questions were also probing, but seemed to be finding the answers they wanted.

Miss Withers gently brought their visit to a close. There must have been some sort of a coded signal they had discussed before leaving their office, because Miss Withers tapped a glass to get everybody's attention and announced that the Board would recommend the use of the facilities.

There were handshakes all around, and Miriam could not stop hugging everyone. After the guests had left, Tom punched the air and said, "We did it!"

The tutorial services proved to be a resounding financial and academic success. The Passover Club had a roof over their heads, a profession they loved and a healthy income. They never forgot the charity that had supported them over the years and gave them a generous monthly donation.

Tom used a portion of the building for his continuing etiquette sessions. A table was permanently laid out behind a fold-away screen with a white dust sheet draped over the crockery and utensils. On the wall he hung his butcher boy's bike, as a reminder of how it had all started.

He kept his eye on the political scene while doing his degree and closely followed the way that the UK may join the European Common Market. While visiting the Jacobs, he sat down with Miriam and Lionel and started to plant a seed about a foreign-language tutorial service.

"Bruchale, does your brain ever stop working?" said Miriam, pinching his cheek.

"I think there will be lots of businesses that will want their sales people learning some languages to export and import goods to this new market," Tom said. "We can offer multiple courses at a time, each lasting several weeks; that way, we can be paid fifty per cent upfront and the balance at the end of their course. We must have a strict timetable for these courses during the day to ensure students arrive on time. No latecomers, as this will disrupt the session and no refund on that session.

"Sammy has another vacant shop a few doors further down the High Street, away from the main hustle and bustle. I am sure he would be interested in us renting it. The Passover Club have the contacts in the university to employ language graduates with good degrees. Most of these graduates are bilingual; some have up to three foreign languages they could teach, to supply our tutorial service. We already have a system working that is tried and tested. So, what do you think?"

Miriam and Lionel looked at each other with a smile and said, "Let's go for it."

Sammy was more than happy to rent out the premises. He even offered six months' rent-free. All the other terms remained the same as the tutorial premises.

Miriam arranged for flyers offering a range of tutorial European language courses to be printed by Mauri Goldstein. The response from various import/export companies was staggering.

Tom called a meeting between the Passover Club, Anja and the Jacobs to discuss the new foreign language tutorial service. It was decided that Anja was going to need assistance in coordinating the appointments and the general logistics of running two tutorial operations.

Gus—or Mr Bentley, as he went by now—offered to continue being the link between the university and the foreign language tutorial services. The young graduates were keen as mustard to demonstrate their skills to the enrolled business members. The business members were very keen to start learning and building relationships with European companies.

Mr Bentley also made enquiries with the university legal department to find out about any law firms that dealt with European contract law. He felt that this would add value to the tutorial service.

The business students soon developed a pattern. They knew that they must not miss their tutorial slot for the lectures, so they would arrive early at Jacob's Café for a coffee and a bagel and stroll a few yards down the road to the tutorial premises. This brought increased business for Miriam and Lionel and extra tips for the servers. Miriam and Lionel kept a section of the café specifically for the business students so her regular customers did not even notice they were there.

These were happy and prosperous times for everybody who had a connection with the tutorial services.

Graduation day arrived; Tom had gained an upper 2:1.

Only two tickets per family were allowed into the graduation hall. These were given to Grandad and Aunt Anja. Both had tears in their eyes when Tom went up on the stage to receive his degree.

Waiting outside were the Passover Club, Tiggy, Miriam and Lionel. They all cheered and clapped as Tom walked towards them with Grandad and Anja by his side.

Miriam made an announcement: "Everybody must come to the café at ten o'clock on Sunday morning. We'll have a private party to celebrate this day. No excuses."

For the party, Miriam and Lionel had laid out a beautiful buffet counter. The café was full of people mingling around: The Passover Club, Tiggy and members of her staff. The Danish consul and his wife. Sammy, Mauri and Benny the tailor. The rabbi and his wife. Miriam and Lionel even tracked down Mr Scrivens, who sold the butcher boy's bike to Grandad.

Tom made a small announcement.

"To some of you, I am Tom. To others, I am Bruchale." Miriam put her handkerchief to her tear-laden eyes at that. "And to others, I am Mr Tomas Larsen, but to me you are my family, and I cannot thank you enough for all the help you have given me over the years. Thank you."

There were cheers and clapping all around the café.

Tea and coffee were served continuously throughout the buffet, which finished about noon, to allow for the Jacobs' Jewish customers to enter the café at two o'clock. This was the time set on Sundays for the Jewish community by law. All other shops were closed due to a ban on Sunday trading.

CHAPTER 25
TOM TAKES AN EDUCATION OFFICER POST AT THE LOCAL PRISON

Everybody was shocked when Tom took up a post at the local prison, mainly from a safety point of view. Almost everybody asked the same question: What made you decide to teach there? And he gave the same reply.

"I made a promise to my former school teacher Mr Montague Foxhall-Trott that if ever I gained a position where I could help people less fortunate than myself, then for a period, I will help those people."

The governor of the prison was a George Parry. He was a firm believer in the idea that education gives people the chance to make better decisions. This was one of the main reasons Tom agreed to the post.

Tom chatted to him about how Foxhall-Trott had changed the lives of the pupils in his class, including himself, by teaching them life skills and how he would like to replicate that with inmates. The governor asked Tom how he proposed to do that and what additional facilities would be required, bearing in mind safety and, more importantly, security.

Tom said he would research some children's toy manufactures to see if moulded rubber crockery and utensils could be made to serve this purpose.

Tom asked the governor if he could have a sign over the classroom door and, possibly inside, to at least make the area appear more educational focused. He would like to call it "The Foxhall-Trott Academy".

"Tom, I have no objection whatsoever to that. I will ask our prison maintenance man, Korky, to come and see you and then you can tell him what you want."

"Why is he called Korky?" asked Tom.

"He was a cat burglar before he went straight, so he became known in prison as Korky the Cat. Believe it or not, his real name is Sidney Snatchit, but you must pronounce it with two syllables."

Tom chuckled with George as he said it.

"He pulls his locked toolbox on wheels around everywhere. He is a brilliant problem-solver and has saved us many thousands of pounds over the years. He takes out one tool at a time and locks the box. Security is paramount here, Tom."

"There is another thing, George. Notebooks. Can I have a supply of notebooks and pencils for the inmates?"

"Of course, Tom, but the notebooks cannot have a wired spine. They will have to have the pages gummed in, because the little blighters will have the wire out and use them for picking locks."

Tom said, "I can see I have a lot to learn. And what about the pencils?"

"No problem," said George. "But they can only be four inches long. A long, sharp pencil could do a lot of damage."

Korky eventually rolled up with his tool trolley. "How can I help, Mr Larsen?"

Korky looked nothing like what Tom imagined a cat burglar would look like. He was in his early sixties, about six foot tall, very thin, with closely cropped black hair. His skin was very pale, presumably from his previous years spent in prison. He had wide eyes with very dark pupils and his nose was quite flat, possibly due to brawling, or not escaping blows due to poor footwork when boxing. Beneath his nose was a black moustache that had no style to it but grew sideways like a cat's.

"Korky, I would prefer to be called Tom amongst staff."

"Ok, Tom, how can I help?"

Tom explained that he would like two signs made, one to display "The Foxhall-Trott Academy" over the entrance door and one internally, above the blackboard. "You can paint them as bold as you like, so long as they look like you are entering a professional establishment."

"Blimey," said Korky. "Are you going to teach these old lags to become educated?"

"Believe it or not, Korky, some of these old lags are already well-educated but in a different way to how we perceive education."

"I will draw you a sketch, Tom, and you can let me know if you like them or wish to change them. I will then make it and put them up for your academy students." He winked as he said it.

"Thank you, Korky."

Korky was very skilled. The signs looked fantastic and created the impression Tom desired.

About seventy per cent of Tom's students just wanted an excuse not to be doing other unpleasant duties, but they were not disruptive. The remaining few had a genuine interest in wanting to better themselves.

Tom wanted to get more inmates to genuinely engage in education for their own benefit and their families'. So, he asked the governor who he thought was the worst repeat offender and the person the other inmates looked up to as their role model.

He did not have to think more than a second. "Billy Garnet, without a doubt. He goes by the name of Biffo. He is loved and hated in equal measures."

"Do you think I can have a meeting with Billy in his cell?"

"Are you serious, Tom? He is not the type of person that likes cosy chats." The governor sighed. "Ok, Tom, if that is want you want. I will arrange that when I can spare two warders to be present outside the cell should anything kick off."

This arranged meeting with Biffo took several weeks to set up.

Tom went along to his cell with the warders who put the cell key into the door and were about to open it when Tom stopped them.

"Please," said Tom.

He knocked on the cell door and said, "Mr Garnet, I am Tomas Larsen. This is where I earn my living and I understand you do the same. May I come in?

The warders turned the cell door key, and Biffo opened the door fully. He stood at about six foot six, very muscular with short black hair and a walrus-style moustache. He was a few years older than Tom, probably in his early thirties. His eyes were dark brown with a stare that had a lot of anger in it. His cell was exceptionally neat and tidy with everything in its place.

Tom asked Biffo if he may take a seat.

"The furniture is not mine," came the reply.

Tom asked the warders, "Would you mind stepping outside the cell and closing the door so that I can talk in private with Mr Garnet? We would both appreciate that."

The warders were confused. "We are concerned about you, Mr Larsen."

"I will take full responsibility. I am sure Mr Garnet does not wish to offer his services here any longer than he needs to."

This brought a slight smile to Biffo's face.

"Look," said Tom, once the warders had left them alone. "I have no advice to offer you on the best way to rob a bank and get away with it, but I am sure there is nobody in this prison that can convince you that they have." This brought another smile to Biffo's face. "I have come here to bore you with my school days with a schoolmaster named Mr Montague Foxhall-Trott."

Biffo's eyebrows rose. He must have thought, *Well, at least it's not somebody who's going to point out the errors of my ways.*

Tom explained Mr Foxhall-Trott was a former public school teacher with sartorial elegance and a cream-coloured Silver Ghost Rolls Royce that he parked next to the other teachers' bikes. Biffo found that very amusing, to the point of laughing out loud.

Tom started to tell him about how Foxhall-Trott had wanted his class of pupils to stand out from the rest of the school just by having attention to detail about their uniforms. He described in detail how he made those changes that cost their parents no extra money. Tom knew that tidiness was an important part of Biffo's life.

When he was done, Tom stood up and thanked Biffo for welcoming into his cell.

Biffo in turn asked Tom if he could come back on another day and tell him more about this Foxhall-Trott bloke.

"I will," said Tom.

"When?"

"Same time next week, if your diary is free." Tom smiled.

Biffo just nodded with a smile on his face. "I look forward to it."

The two warders that stood outside Biffo's cell were amazed that Tom was having a conversation with Biffo and that there were sounds of laughter coming from the cell.

Tom explained to Biffo that both his parents died during an influenza epidemic, and it was his grandfather and widowed aunt Anja who had brought him up with lots of love and encouragement. On hearing this, Biffo took Tom into his confidence about his childhood. He said his alcoholic father left the home when he was ten years old and his wonderful mother had to work three jobs to pay bills and put food on the table. He explained that missing school and mixing with the wrong crowd got him into trouble. He also mentioned that his writing and reading skills were virtually non-existent.

"That is the least of your problems, Biffo," Tom told him. "I can help you with that, here in your furnished flat."

With that remark, Biffo laughed out loud.

"If you do not mind," said Tom, "I would prefer to call you Mr Garnet, because that is the respect you deserve. I will see you next week and we will start on your reading and writing skills."

"What did you do to make him speak to you and get an amusing response?" enquired the warders, when Tom left the cell.

"I just treated him like any other human being," replied Tom.

The prison governor invited Tom to his office to find out what reaction Biffo had had to his visit.

"It all went well, George. In fact, he is happy for me to visit him next week."

"That is excellent. Mr Garnet has a disruptive influence on a lot of the inmates that look up to him as their leader, and no matter what systems we use to change the situation, it always ends up with privileges being removed."

The word soon travelled around the prison about this Larsen bloke and the fact that Biffo liked him. Tom noticed that the inmates who now attended his class were more attentive—or at least they sat and looked interested, and some even started to asked questions. Tom's Confucius plaque seemed to be having some effect.

Over the coming weeks, Tom had several more meetings in Biffo's cell. He contacted Tiggy and asked for suggestions on suitable reading material on learning maths and reading. She selected just two books on each subject and put them out on an extended loan to Tom.

The following weeks, Tom was accompanied by only one warder, who waited outside to ensure privacy for Tom and Biffo.

Over a period of twelve weeks, Biffo gained enough confidence to understand basic maths and to read up to a certain level. Tom was a natural teacher. During that time, Tom discussed with Biffo how listening to Foxhall-Trott and learning about etiquette had broken down barriers and the mystique about how the upper and middle classes conducted themselves, in both dress and dining.

Tom went on to tell Biffo that Foxhall-Trott had taught him that knowledge can open many doors and that was how he had started his three businesses.

Tom looked at Biffo and said, "So why am I working in a prison as an education officer, when I have three very profitable businesses? Do you keep promises, Mr Garnet?"

"To my mother, yes, but to others sometimes."

"I told you how Foxhall-Trott sadly died. I made him a promise that, for a while, I will offer help to those less fortunate than myself. So, now you know."

Tom was taken aback as Biffo suddenly stood up and approached him with his arms outstretched, placing them around Tom's shoulders, giving Tom a hug.

Tom thought, for a moment, that it must have been the first time in quite a while that Biffo had put his arms around someone's shoulders without meaning to harm them.

George Parry called Tom to his office and sat him down. "Tom, I have had a request from Mr Billy Garnet to attend your education class."

"Good news," replied Tom. "I am sure he will benefit."

"We have also had a request for another ten inmates who want to attend. This is probably because they want to be seen with Biffo Garnet."

"That is fine, but I think that will have to be the cut-off point for now until you can find me more accommodation, George."

"Things are looking up, Tom, but let us see how this goes first and then we can review the situation."

Tom had a class of about twenty inmates in the education room. He went around the room asking their names. He came to the first one who stood up and said, "Robin Hood, Mr Larsen."

Biffo turned around in his seat and just fixed the inmate with a glare. The inmate stood up again and gave his actual name followed by "Mr Larsen."

While looking at the inmate, Biffo said, very quietly, "Sir."

The inmate stood up and quickly repeated it. "Sorry, Mr Larsen, sir."

Tom said, "I would prefer if you all addressed each other by 'Mister' followed by the surname. I think this is more formal and respectful. You may call me sir."

Tom then pointed to the Confucius plaque and said, "Gentlemen, please do not be afraid to follow that advice. It is over two thousand five hundred years old, and is still relevant today.

"I will also give you another piece of good advice by a Chinese philosopher named Lao Tzu. 'A journey of a thousand miles begins with a single step.' You, gentlemen, have taken that first step, and please believe me when I tell you that each and every one of you has a special talent outside the criminal world. We will all discover that as we progress."

He then went on to set out what he would be teaching, covering basic education and life skills.

"What do you mean life skills?" enquired one of the inmates.

"To put it in a nutshell, Mr Taylor," said Tom, "it is all the things you may think that only middle- and upper-class people know about. So, I intend to unlock all the mystique about that so that you are no different to them, except maybe financially."

"What is mystique?" asked another inmate.

"Mr Roberts, Confucius is working well this session."

This raised some quiet laughter.

"It is another word for something that is shrouded in mystery."

"Thank you, sir," came the reply.

Tom then went on to basic education matters to assess what level the inmates were at. At the end of the session, he asked some of the inmates to remain behind, but not Biffo.

"You may have wondered why I have asked this group to remain behind," he told the group at the end of the session. "You, gentlemen, are the uncut diamonds of education and together you will be turned into brilliant, polished diamonds."

The group turned and just looked at each other, wondering what Tom meant.

"Thank you, gentlemen, for your attentiveness, and I will see you at the next group meeting."

At the next meeting, Tom started by talking about the Royal Navy in the 1700s and how scurvy had plagued sailors for centuries, making them become very ill and possibly die. He told them it was discovered that by giving sailors doses of lemon and lime juice, they gradually became well.

"That is why some Americans call us Limeys," he said. "The first sailors that were treated became well again and then helped the others until they were well enough and could continue with their duties. The point I am making, gentlemen, is that we will all have some degree of scurvy on this voyage together, so we will all help each other until each crew member is fit and well. Do I have your agreement on that?"

"Yes, sir," came the resounding reply.

"You will notice that I have rearranged your seating places, because we want to help anybody who may require a little help. Please do not forget that the person you help today may be giving you help tomorrow."

At first, the classmates thought the idea of calling each other "Mister" was a bit ridiculous, but they gradually realised that it created a level playing field in the room and treated everybody with respect.

Over a period of months, the basic education standards started to improve. Some of the inmates were visiting the library and asking the trustee librarian for more educational texts.

Tom knew that his time with the inmates should not be totally about basic education. There has to be a mixture of life skills to keep an interest going. Over a period of several months, in between the basic education lessons, Tom wanted to introduce life skills to the inmates.

The inmates arrived as usual on their designated day and sat ready to learn more about basic education. Tom had a dust sheet draped over an object in the front of the class. The inmates were looking at each other, trying to guess what was beneath it.

"When you first joined, I mentioned life skills," said Tom. "So, I thought it would be a good idea to start showing you how upper- and middle-class men would dress. Gentlemen, wait for it—there is an important word coming up. Sartorial. The word is a tailoring expression, relating to a smartly dressed person."

Tom then looked at two of the inmates seated in the front row and, with an eye and hand gesture, asked them to come forward and remove the dust sheets together to reveal what is underneath.

The dustsheets were removed, and facing the class was a manikin dressed in a formal suit. By the side of this on a stand stood a white shirt, a detachable shirt collar and a tie.

"Gentlemen, we are going to explore this style of dress and learn how to wear it. And just before any of you think you are looking at your breakout suit..." Tom swivelled the manikin around to show that Benny had embroidered in thick white cotton "CALL POLICE ESCAPED CONVICT". This brought howls of laughter from the inmates.

"Gentlemen, I have an interesting idea for you. It is said that justice may not be about justice at all. It may be about he who tells the best story and wears the finest clothes."

The inmates could relate to that statement, and some were making quiet remarks about their defence counsel and the prosecutors they had faced during their lifetime.

"That is why it is important to know how to present yourself. I have this dressed manikin on loan from a very good tailor friend of mine. We'll start by talking about the right fabric and what you should spent your hard-earned cash on—or, as it may be, somebody else's hard-earned cash."

Some of the inmates concealed a smile beneath a cupped hand over their mouth.

Benny the tailor had given Tom a list of pointers of what to look out for when choosing fabric for a garment. Tom relayed these to his students, asking them to write them down.

"Any help with spelling, just shout out," he told them. "Let us start with hardness. This makes the cloth sleeker and smoother. A worsted wool is the best for this. It will make a suit that can last for many years.

"Crispness. This makes the cloth feel dryer and will maintain the creases longer, particularly important in trousers.

"Nap. This sounds a rather funny word, but what you are looking for is how hairy the cloth is. The length of the nap relates to the hardness and softness of the cloth. Use the flat palm of your hand to smooth the cloth; that will tell you the direction of the weave.

"Weight. One of the most important things to look out for. Remember, the heavier the weight in ounces, the better the fabric will hang and it will wear better.

"Take your selected cloths out into the daylight and check the colours. They may look entirely different than they did in the shop lighting.

"Sleeve length. The sleeve length should be cut to show a quarter to half inch of the shirt cuff.

"Finally, take your time. You are making a big investment. That suit and your appearance could get you the job you want."

Tom invited the inmates to come close to the manikin and feel the texture of the cloth and inspect the quality of the stitching. He then told them to look at the trousers. They were narrow in style with no turn-ups. A small slit each side allowed the front to drape over the shoelaces, while the rear section covered part of the heel. He said, "This helps to maintain the crease in the trousers, rather than giving a sagging appearance to the lower leg of the trouser."

Tom then turned to the collarless shirt on the stand. "How many of you have worn one of these?"

No hands were raised.

"How many of you have seen these before?"

Many hands were raised.

"Where have you seen them?" enquired Tom.

Several replies came back almost simultaneously. Grandfather, father, uncle.

"Well, as gentlemen, I think you should know how to put them together."

Tom asked the group to gather around him.

"In my hand I have two collar studs. The smaller one fits into the small slit on the back of the shirt collar rim with the small brass stud facing outwards. You then put the shirt on and put the longer collar stud through the top button hole, pulling each shirt section together with the swivel brass stud facing outwards.

"Now we have the tricky job of attaching the shirt collar with the tie to the shirt. This takes practice. I would recommend that you use a silk necktie if possible because it glides more easily within the detachable collar. While holding the detachable collar in your left hand, open out the collar and place the necktie along the central joint of the collar, making sure that the wide part of the tie is on the right-hand side. On the narrow left-hand side of the tie, you will see a diagonal join within the tie. This diagonal joint should be about two inches below the end of the collar. This is the part of the tie where you will start to form your tie knot.

"You may require assistance attaching the collar to the shirt, but with practice you should be able to undertake this by yourself. While holding the tie sandwiched between the collar, feel for the small stud at the back of the shirt and fasten the collar to it. Bring both ends of the collar to the front collar stud while still holding the tie in place, and button it through onto the shirt.

"As explained earlier, with the tie hanging down in front of you, place the longer side over the shorter side at the diagonal marker point and form the knot of your choice. Finally, make sure that no tie is showing below the collar.

"I think cuff links should be worn rather than a buttoned cuff, but the choice is yours."

Tom was very keen to get the inmates interested in etiquette. The thought behind this was that maybe some of the inmates could get a position in hospitality when they were released. He also felt that learning about this subject removed the stigma about being ignorant when a formal dining experience occurred.

George was fully on board with this idea. Finally, they had found a manufacturer that would tool up a production of flexible plastic crockery, wine and champagne goblets plus utensils. This manufacturer surprised George and Tom by stating that, provided he stamps his company name on every article and considering why they are doing it, the goods were free.

The goods arrived in two large boxes. Tom asked Korky, as an ex-inmate, to advise him on ways to make sure that none of the goods went missing, because there would be a lot on display while demonstrating to his inmates and getting them involved.

"That is easy," said Korky. "All we must do is stencil in bright yellow the shape of the article on the table, and if it is removed the yellow marker will be on show."

"So simple but effective. You are a genius, Korky."

"I know," he replied.

At a weekly meeting with George, Tom would discuss who was being released from prison in the coming weeks. This gave him the opportunity to concentrate on those inmates regarding their basic education and now etiquette. This was in the hope that they would take a different direction when they left the prison gates and went back into society.

The demonstrations in etiquette were, at first, treated with suspicion, but Tom's teaching skills, and particularly on this subject, were outstanding. The inmates could all recall at some point in their life how they and members of their family had been embarrassed when they did not know how to conduct themselves.

The demonstrations and participation gave so much confidence to the inmates. They would meticulously write down in their notebooks every action and diagram, as Tom had instructed. They would take it in turns to be the server or customer, with the remainder of the class as onlookers watching every detail as the scene unfolded. Tom had taught them not to shout out when something was not correct but to note it and, if called upon, give their interpretation of what should have happened instead.

This seemed to be a wonderful way of learning the subject.

Tom had designed certificates for those who reached a standard that he felt would qualify them to work in hospitality. He discussed in detail the design of this certificate with George. The heading had "The Foxhall-Trott Academy" written on it, and the certificate went on to say that: *"The holder of this certificate... NAME...DATE... has attained a high standard in etiquette to serve High Teas and Fine Dining. Signed by Tomas Larsen BA (Hons) HMP DUXTON."*

George questioned if the certificate should mention the prison. Tom felt it was essential that the document should be honest and any employer should know exactly who they were giving an opportunity to.

The Prison Board were aware of the work that both George and Tom were doing with the inmates, and the fact that the offenders who had been on that course were likely not to reoffend.

Their approval for the life skills course was given initially for a period of one year, with a stipulation that the receiving employer should be asked to give feedback so that the Board can judge the merits of the programme.

Tom could see in every inmate that their confidence was growing daily. This was probably the only chance they'd had in their lives of achieving a worthwhile certificate that could prove they were good at something.

During the early years, Billy "Biffo" Garnet became a devoted disciple of Tom's, and although it took him almost two years to achieve his certificate, it was framed and placed in pride of place on his cell wall. Upon his release, he asked if there was any possibility that he could assist Tom with his work.

George took this request very seriously, because Biffo Garnet was one of the most disruptive inmates he'd had in his prison for a very long time. George could see what a positive effect Tom's Foxhall-Trott Academy had had on so many former inmates passing out through the prison gates.

He brought up Biffo Garnet's request at his weekly meeting with Tom.

"I was shocked," said George. "I thought after serving ten years, not counting all the previous years he spent in this prison, he would be delighted to see the back of the place."

"I would be delighted to have him as my assistant education officer, George, if you can manage it in your budget."

"Well, there have been tremendous benefits in you running these lectures, Tom. Damaged property is virtually nil and the prison has been much calmer, making the staff very happy. I will put it to the Prison Board and see if they approve. If they do, then hopefully they will also fund that position."

It took several weeks for the Board to reply. George invited Tom to his office so that he could be present when the reply letter was opened.

Dear Mr Parry,

Thank you for your letter requesting an additional post within the Foxhall-Trott Academy.

We have followed with great interest the progress of this original pilot scheme in showing former inmates new skills to take with them upon their release.

It is something the Board would like to consider establishing in other prisons and would welcome any suggestions you may have on how we could achieve this at low cost.

Regarding the post you requested, we have no objection and have decided that additional funds will be made available to meet the funding of that post.

In addition, we will also provide a one-off payment of £10,000 to be utilised in the Prison Education Department. Receipts for all disbursement are to be forwarded to us for payment.

The Board wish you well in your endeavours and look forward to any recommendations you may have in expanding this project to other prisons.

Yours sincerely,
Ernest Trubshaw.
Chairman of the Prison Board.

George and Tom were ecstatic with the contents of the reply letter and could not wait to inform Mr Garnet that he was now holder of the post "Assistant Education Officer in the Prison Service".

Mr Garnet never seemed to lose the smile he attained when he was first told that he had got the job working with Tom.

He proved to be an excellent and patient teacher. Not only that, but he was also always looking for fresh ideas, having a good insight into how the inmates were thinking. An idea that he came up with was to turn prison roles on their head. He mentioned to Tom that inmates looked at warders as controllers of their life, and it would break down tensions between the two if the inmates were to reverse the roles.

Tom asked, "How?"

"During the etiquette lessons, the inmates watch and judge each other, and that is how we learn. How about if we could ask warders to take part as the customers? We could have a mock menu and the service could be carried out according to the menu. The warders are getting a free tuition in fine dining, and the inmates are in control by showing and correcting what that are doing wrong in a polite environment."

"I think that is a brilliant idea, Biffo. I will have a word with the governor and see what he thinks."

"While you're in his office, Tom, what about asking him to send Jerome Winston Tate out as our ambassador to show other prisons how we do it in Duxton? I am sure the governor is aware that in prisons there is a code of respectability between the inmates, with safecrackers and unarmed bank robbers at the top, while the lowest are paedophiles, who are loathed in bucketloads.

"Jerome has all the credentials. He was a former public school pupil, he breezed the basic education, life skills and etiquette certificate, he has a charming manner and is a well-respected safecracker. He is known in the criminal world as Dr Tate."

"Why Dr Tate?"

"He had a doctor's stethoscope adapted with hearing aid amplifiers so that he could hear the safe barrels tumble and click when turning the dial on the safe to open it. He has never been caught; he was picked out in an identity parade. The term that he is serving is for not disclosing where he has hidden his loot.

"Tom this also fulfils the Prison Board's request to take the Foxhall-Trott Academy into other prisons."

"Genius, Biffo, that's genius."

Jerome was a lovable rogue. He was very tall and always immaculately turned out, even in prison clothing. He had straight blonde hair, almost shoulder length, well-groomed, and a pale complexion with blue eyes. His stature was quite thin. He had no objection to prison life; he equated it to boarding school, with the only difference being that the Warders did not speak in Received Pronunciation English. He referred to inmates as "old boy" or his chums.

Tom had welcomed him in his class and retained him there longer than he should have, because of his positive influence on the other inmates. He had an excellent manner of correcting the inmates on their speech and grammar, which was always received in the good humour it was given. Tom thought, like Biffo, that he would make an excellent ambassador for the Foxhall-Trott Academy and Duxton Prison.

This idea was put to George, who invited the principal and supervising warden officers into his office to bounce the idea off them of having the warders be customers in the etiquette lessons. To his surprise, they welcomed the idea and volunteered to be the first. They also supported the idea of Jerome Winston Tate being escorted to various other jails, showing them how they do it at HMP Duxton.

This practice lesson went better than expected, with the other warders putting their names forward for both etiquette lectures and the escorting of Jerome, who was non-violent and very entertaining.

Jerome's tour went on for about six months. In each prison he had his own cell and dined with the warders in their mess room, but the fare was no different to what was served to the inmates, except for the occasional treat when one of the warder's wives had baked a cake that was shared. The Prison Board ensured his contact with inmates during his prison stays was minimal, both for his safety and to avoid Jerome passing on any of his criminal knowledge to other inmates under duress.

This tour made Jerome even more of a celebrity. Upon his return there were plenty of inmates ready and willing to, as Jerome would say, fag for him (a public school term meaning to run errands for someone, iron their clothes, etc.).

CHAPTER 26
LIFE GOES ON

Tom's basic education lessons and life skills were taught at HMP Duxton and other prisons over the next few decades, achieving excellent results.

He was so proud that it was all being carried out under the Foxhall-Trott Academy banner.

However, during this period, he encountered both sadness and joyfulness. Grandad had passed away peacefully due to old age, but not before he was able to give Anja away in marriage to a wonderful widower by the name of Magnus.

Tom also had two previous inmates now running his High Street etiquette lectures to take the pressure off while he continued his prison duties.

Miriam and Lionel had decided to sell the café and retire to Tel Aviv in Israel; this was both a sad and happy occasion. Tom was very tearful throughout the farewell party. He treasured the letters he still received from them both, which always opened with:

Our Dearest Bruchale,
We miss you so much and cannot wait for your visit to us.

Miriam and Lionel had sold their share in the academic and foreign language business to the Passover Club, making Tom and them all equal partners, to Tom's delight.

Tom had been discussing his pending early retirement with George and how they would find a replacement to continue with the Foxhall-Trott Academy. Tom was confident that they would find a suitable person, and he was keen to make sure that Billy "Biffo" Garnet attended any interviews of the candidates. Tom felt that Biffo was a shining example of what his programme could achieve, and to know that Biffo could work with his replacement was important. George fully endorsed that sentiment.

A replacement was selected: Jerome Winston Tate, who applied and beat all the other candidates hands down on qualifications and experience of the prison environment. When he'd been released from prison a few years before, he'd decided to work with charities that helped former inmates.

Tom and George chuckled at the thought that inmates attending the Foxhall-Trott Academy under Jerome Winston Tate's leadership would all leave prison with a Received Pronunciation accent.

With a suitable replacement found, Tom could now turn his attention to matters that had been left on hold while carrying out his duties in prison. One of those was to visit his beloved Miriam and Lionel in Tel Aviv. Travel arrangements were made and the adventure began.

Miriam and Lionel were waiting for him at the arrivals gate. Tom was pulling his suitcase. He did not have to look for them; Miriam was gesturing people to move out of the way while she tried to reach her Bruchale.

"Lionel, the suitcase! Take the suitcase."

Miriam held on to her Bruchale for what seemed a lifetime, and as soon as she released her grip, Lionel was there.

Tears were flowing down everyone's cheeks as they walked to a waiting car. Miriam could not stop looking at Tom, hugging him and squeezing his cheek.

"You look so pale from being in that prison!"

Lionel held her hand and said, "Miriam, if you talk like that outside this car, people will think that Bruchale has just been released from prison."

Miriam took her floral handkerchief from her pocket and held it to her mouth. "Oy vey, what am I saying, Lionel."

Everybody started to laugh, just like the old days.

Tom spent six glorious weeks with Miriam and Lionel. They took their Bruchale around to every friend and neighbour they knew in Israel as though Tom was the Prodigal Son who had returned home. Tom was taken to every historical site and even went through the Negev Desert to the resort of Eilat on the Red Sea.

The departure was as tearful as the arrival, with everybody promising that they would meet again. Sadly, the following year, Miriam and Lionel both passed away within three months of each other. Tom was sure one followed the other because of a broken heart.

He sent a letter to be read by members at the Shiva, saying how these beautiful people had given him his start in life and treated him as a member of their family and that for him, this was like losing his parents all over again.

It took Tom over a year to adjust to the fact that Miriam and Lionel would no longer be part of his life. Both parties had always looked forward to receiving letters, updating each other about what was happening in their lives.

To take his mind off his sad loss, Tom concentrated on the next duty he wanted to fulfil. A promise he had made when he was in senior school.

He would visit the grave of his mentor, Montague Foxhall-Trott, in the South of France, who had tragically died due to a road accident in the village of le Soleilville.

Tom wanted to experience, as far as possible, the same experience Foxhall-Trott would have had driving his Rolls Royce through France on the way to the family's gîte in the South of France. Sammy Kaye and Benny the tailor heard about Tom's quest and surprised him with a solution. One of their business contacts ran a wedding car business that had a cream vintage Rolls Royce like the one Foxhall-Trott had driven, but it would not be available for another two months, after the wedding season had eased off.

Everybody in the Jewish community was aware how Bruchale had contributed to the pushke box over many years, and now it was time to give a little back.

Sammy and Benny had put the offer of the hire car to Tom, with the only stipulation being that he paid for all the expenses of the travel, including the insurance to drive the Rolls Royce in France for a period of ten days.

Tom was deliriously happy that he had a chance to fulfil the promise he had made. He had never dreamt it would be in this style.

His thoughts turned to Biffo, who was a product of what Foxhall-Trott had wanted him to achieve by educating the under-privileged and making them valued citizens. He put the idea to Biffo of travelling to France with him. Biffo was excited about the idea because he had never travelled further than thirty miles from his home. George and Jerome, his new boss, were delighted at the prospect of Biffo seeing a bit of the world. They were keen to be involved, sorting out his new passport and currency for the trip.

Tom received several lessons from the wedding car hire company on how to drive the Rolls Royce, whenever it was not in business use.

The big day arrived, and both Tom and Biffo set off in this magnificent car. A large crowd turned out for their send-off. There were members of the Jewish community and the Passover Club, including Aunt Anja and her new husband, Magnus. Biffo had a beaming smile from ear to ear. He felt like royalty.

Tom had always known that he wanted his drive down to the South of France to be as close as possible to the route that Foxhall-Trott would have taken. There would have been no motorways or tolls during that period. Tom wanted to experience the same sights, villages and towns that his mentor would have passed through.

Tom had asked the advice of a motoring organisation before he left the UK, asking them the most likely route that would have been taken from Calais to St Tropez during the 1950s. They were kind enough to provide Tom with a print of a route that would be a close match to what he was trying to achieve. This route basically took him from Calais to Rouen, bypassed Paris, onward to Orléans and Chartres, driving south to Clermont-Ferrand, Orange, Avignon, Aix-en-Provence and finally St Tropez, with about a twenty-mile end-of-the-journey drive to le Soleilville.

Tom and Biffo were so excited about the places they stayed and the sites they saw on the way down to their destination. Once they had travelled across the Channel by ferry, they soon became accustomed to the crowds that gathered around the car when they had a meal in a small village. A small crowd would always gather and take photographs of themselves beside the car, or just stand and admire it.

In le Soleilville, Tom pulled the Rolls Royce alongside a small car park next to what seemed to be the only café in the village. The presence of the car started to attract its usual small crowd, including many children. They both entered the café and ordered an evening meal and something to drink. They also wanted to find out information on where the church was, and a bed and breakfast to spend a night or two.

The café owner introduced herself as Annebelle and she started to talk about the car. She said a car just like the one parked outside used to visit the village every summer. It was owned by an Englishman who would teach any of the villagers who wished to learn to speak English. She said her parents had owned this café then and would send her over as a young girl to the orchard with other villagers to learn English during the summer months.

Tom explained why he was in the village and asked Annebelle what she remembered about Foxhall-Trott.

"He was such a kind and beautiful person," she told him. "My mother said he would visit the café at the same time each morning and order a black coffee and a pain au chocolat. He would then pull a watch on a chain from his pocket and would wait until it was the exact time to leave. My mother said he was not crazy, but you have another word for this."

"Eccentric!" said Tom.

"Yes," said Annebelle, "that is the word. Everybody in the village loved him and called him Professeur Trott. My mother was there that terrible day when he left the café and was knocked down by a truck. So very sad. He is buried in our church graveyard."

Tom asked Annebelle if she could find them a place to stay for two nights, because they wanted to visit his grave and look at the gîte that had been his family's holiday home.

"While you are finishing your meal, I will make some phone calls," she told them.

Annebelle called her assistant to look after the café. She then picked up her bicycle and said, "Follow me in your car." She took them to the village square and introduced them to the owners of a small but very clean pension.

As she was leaving, she said, "I will meet you at the café at ten o'clock tomorrow, and I will show you where he rests."

The next morning, Annebelle was waiting in her café as promised, and they all drove up to the church in the Rolls Royce. To Tom and Biffo's surprise, there was quite a gathering of people carrying flowers, with the priest leading the crowd and singing hymns.

This was a very emotional moment for Tom as they alighted from the car. The crowd parted as the threesome approached the priest. He indicated with his hand the gravestone of Montague Foxhall-Trott. Tom could see that the grave had been well looked after over the years. Annebelle told him that the villagers put fresh flowers on it every other day and clean the black marble headstone.

Tom placed a small black marble plaque with the inscription:
This mentor enriched my life so that I may share my knowledge with others.

The crowd clapped as Tom placed the plaque down and Annebelle explained to the crowd want the inscription meant. They all passed their flowers to Tom to place on the grave.

Biffo put his arm around Tom's shoulder and said, "Tom, you have certainly carried out the words you had inscribed on the plaque."

"He was a wonderful man, Biffo, a wonderful man."

Annebelle guided them back to the village and the café. "Come, I will show you where he taught us English."

Across the road from the café was the orchard were Foxhall-Trott had voluntarily taught his English class. Annebelle pointed to two oak posts with holes ascending both posts. "He would put oak pegs into these holes to hold his blackboard. You can see that the villagers have beautifully painted these posts in memory of Professeur Trott.

"I will now show you the family gîte he used every summer."

It was just as Tom imagined: stone built with a tiled roof with two dormer windows. The windows of the gîte were small and square with weathered wooden shutters each side to block out the heat of the midday sun. The wooden front door looked as old as the gîte.

"I hope you will share a meal this evening in my café with some of the villagers, before your long journey home tomorrow," said Annebelle.

Tom and Biffo enjoyed a wonderful meal amongst people who'd also known Foxhall-Trott, just like he had known him.

The journey back was just as exciting for both the travellers.

Upon his return, Tom thought long and hard over the autumn and winter months about what the next chapter in his life would bring. His mind kept returning to that village in the South of France and the kindness of the villagers, in particular Annebelle, and a comment Biffo had made on the return journey: "I can see why Foxhall-Trott loved the people in that village."

***

If you travel to the South of France and have a chance to visit a charming village about twenty miles from St Tropez called le Soleilville, and when the blossom arrives on the fruit trees in the orchard, you will find an elderly man with grey hair teaching a small group of children English, reciting from a blackboard. This elderly man, called Professeur Larsen, married a local woman called Annebelle and they have two grown-up children, a son and a daughter named Montague and Miriam.

THE END

What Did You Think of *The Foxhall-Trott Pupil?*

A big thank you for purchasing this book. It means a lot that you chose this book specifically from such a wide range on offer. I do hope you enjoyed it.

Book reviews are incredibly important for an author. All feedback helps them improve their writing for future projects and for developing this edition. If you are able to spare a few minutes to post a review on Amazon, that would be much appreciated.

Publisher Information

Rowanvale Books provides publishing services to independent authors, writers and poets all over the globe. We deliver a personal, honest and efficient service that allows authors to see their work published, while remaining in control of the process and retaining their creativity. By making publishing services available to authors in a cost-effective and ethical way, we at Rowanvale Books hope to ensure that the local, national and international community benefits from a steady stream of good quality literature.

For more information about us, our authors or our publications, please get in touch.

www.rowanvalebooks.com
info@rowanvalebooks.com

www.ingramcontent.com/pod-product-compliance
Lightning Source LLC
Chambersburg PA
CBHW041140170626
46815CB00007B/337

* 9 7 8 1 8 3 5 8 4 0 0 4 7 *